THE
GIRL
From Colombia

THE
GIRL
From Colombia

Dear Taylor -
Your attention to this
book means a lot.
Thank you !!!
Julian

JULIAN RODRIGUEZ

gatekeeper press

Columbus, Ohio

The Girl from Colombia

Published by Gatekeeper Press
2167 Stringtown Rd, Suite 109
Columbus, OH 43123-2989
www.GatekeeperPress.com

The editorial work for this book is entirely the product of the author. Gatekeeper Press did not participate in and is not responsible for any aspect of these elements.

ISBN (paperback): 9781642379426
eISBN: 9781642378900

Writing in 1887, during the time period of this novel, Guy de Maupassant describes the unknown terror that haunts the narrator of his celebrated story Le Horla:

> At first I saw nothing, and then suddenly it appeared to me as if a page of the book...turned over of its own accord... In about four minutes, I saw, I saw...another page lift itself up and fall down on the others, as if a finger had turned it over. My armchair was empty, appeared empty, but I knew that He was there, He, and sitting in my place, and that He was reading. With a furious bound, the bound of an enraged wild beast that wishes to disembowel its tamer, I crossed my room to seize him, to strangle him, to kill him! But before I could reach it, my chair fell over... my window closed as if some thief had been surprised and had fled out into the night, shutting it behind him.

What Maupassant describes appears to be a being of multiple forms: at once a figment of the imagination, a private torment, and an indefinable type of evil that haunts the world, which lies low awaiting the moment to attack. In rational terms, we can think of this evil as simply the force of a person's acts. If one wants to think more mystically, one can see it as an atmosphere suffused with ill will, with ill intentions, even devilish forces.

Something of this same atmosphere pervades the New Jersey of this manuscript. We start with a poisoning attempt by young Isabel, a hinted past of misery, guilt and torture. Things become progressively worse; blades are driven into flesh just as a flash of gold crosses the page, and all of this occurs in what at first seemed to be so civilized a backdrop but is supernatural in its own right.

But evil—or at least criminal acts—cannot, in a dialectical fashion, exist without love and compassion. The romance that flourishes between Joseph and Isabel is a perfect example of this. The kiss with which the novel begins to draw to an end, the strange affection that is communicated—all of this gives us a certain hope, even within such strange proceedings. Sometimes what is invisible to us is, after all, what we need most.

PART ONE

THE
INCOMING
TIDE

Sea Girt, New Jersey

April, 1884

J ust after sunset. One day before the Spring Solstice.

Isabel knew how to move like a small cat. She taught herself this talent when she first arrived at the Johnsons' house: *Move silently, look for shadows, use them as pathways, or caves where you can hide, if need be. But always, always,* she told herself, *move without notice.*

It took her several months to master this, but once she did, she could move about the Johnson house in utter secrecy. Overlooked by the house staff, sometimes she could pass just under their noses without evoking even a glance her way. She did this once—she passed Sarah, the Johnsons' housekeeper, a woman known for her sharp eye, her attention to detail. Isabel's small feet made not one sound as they touched the soft wood floors behind Sarah's broad behind, her cotton skirts flouncing out to the right and left. Isabel slipped behind her, shadowing her as the old woman shifted her weight up the broad staircase to change out the bed linens. Sarah never once felt Isabel's tiny frame passing on the stairs behind her. She never once turned, her eyes never darted back to see what—or who—followed.

Isabel's mouth turned up into a tiny, mischievous smile as she darted to the left when Sarah reached the second-floor landing and moved down the hall to the right, never once noticing the small girl's appearance—and then disappearance.

That was how Isabel knew she could slip the poison into Mr. Johnson's tea without anyone being the wiser. In fact, it delighted her—the idea that she could be inside the kitchen, first in the pantry, and then just inside the broom closet for minutes, all during the bustle when the two cooks and their waitstaff served Mr. Johnson and his guests their baked oysters, roasted peppers, and yams. (Isabel was even able to steal two bubbling, warm oysters off guests' plates before they were served.) After that, she moved about unnoticed as the guests took claret and the fresh peach puddings that had made Sarah famous. Isabel then waited for the house to go slowly, slowly silent again.

Her tummy bristled with excitement. She could feel the tips of her fingers heat up as she let the dusty lye she held inside a pouch slip into his nighttime teacup. She couldn't help but giggle—she had lifted the poison while watching stable boys drift out of the back barn, their faces weak and sour from the scent the lye gave off. Sarah's soap vats were heated up to make the soap cakes and were filled with the poison. They made hundreds of soap cakes every year. They had to; between the work in the orchards and the ironworks plants, they made more grime in a day than all of New York City. The Johnson operation was a dirty one.

No one would miss the small tubs of poison used to keep the vermin away from the livestock. She did not need much. A tiny handful, and no one stopped to think why the tea did not smell of jasmine, nor did they know why it clouded slightly. Last and best, they never saw or heard Isabel's tiny steps.

It was only when Mr. Johnson began to double over in pain, at the end of the moon's arc outside, that anyone began to retrace the events of the evening at all.

I'm only twelve years old, Isabel thought. *Just think what I'll be able to do when I'm sixteen, or eighteen…*

CHAPTER ONE

D r. Edwards was used to being called out at all hours of the night. Ancient citizens of Sea Girt and neighboring towns flopping over the mattress helplessly was a common house call, or they would tumble onto the hard floor and a hip would shatter. Births brought him out often, as did young mothers who knew little about how to cure a wailing child, strange fevers, or the bad effects of a drunken night.

Dr. Edwards' heart did not rise much for any of these things. His heart was sedated, really. It did not beat like timpani the way the hearts of the Edwards' household's women did. He felt a soft, easy detachment toward humans, never loving them enough to feel too much pain, never grieving beyond measure. This dispassion enabled him to remain steady in the room while others yelped, cried, bled, upchucked, and often—angry and scared about the murky future of death—bit. He could eat a meal after a crushed bone surgery. He could sleep after a death. He could even have a glass of whiskey and sleep like a baby after a suicide.

But this call, which came about midnight, was a message that Samuel Johnson was aspirating his meal, his lips blue as the moon, his face and eyes swollen to the size of walnuts, and it nauseated

Edwards. The wagon he banged inside on the journey over gave him a fierce headache; he was red-eyed and sour when he arrived at the Johnsons' front door. He leaned on the doorframe for just a moment to rest before the door flew open and a wide-eyed Sarah, sweating and frantic, pulled her body sideways and then turned her back to him and fled like a rumpled-up old lady up the stairs.

Edwards didn't ask any questions for a moment or so. He paused on the stairs, gazing where Johnson had thrown up his oysters. The second heap of undigested food showed threads of blood in his vomit. It was then that he began to ask Sarah questions.

"Was he ever unconscious, Sarah?"

"No, heaving and retching and gasping for air lots of times. Not able to speak at all—save to say, *'Fuck off!'* quite often. But always alive—groping like an ape, mostly."

"Have you done anything for him? Given him anything to drink, for example?"

"Water. A few tries at that, but he spewed it back up as fast as it hit his lips. I gave him an ice shaving to smooth along his mouth, as his lips are split open, but he tossed the ice glass against the wall."

They reached the master bedroom door—open all the way, which it never was. This was a door the entire staff knew never to pass through without express permission. Edwards sailed through, dodging puke stains littered about the rugs. Johnson himself convulsed like a bird's wing on his side, opening and shutting his arms around his knees as the spasms hit his body, one after the other.

"Hullo, Johnson," Edwards said openly. "Let's try and get you on your stomach to see what can be done." He pulled Samuel Johnson's shoulders apart and tried to lay him flat to examine him, but Johnson's arms, not in his control, smacked Edwards hard across the face.

"Christ!" Edwards barked. Sarah moved to the other side of the bed and held Johnson down. He glanced at the blue lips and then bent to smell one of the freshest piles of puke. The tint of lye made him lurch back slightly. "It's good that you've thrown up a good deal, Sarah says."

Johnson then grabbed Edwards, pulling his face down to meet his mouth. "The letter," he spat into Edwards' ear.

Edwards stood straight. "Yes, I know. You've told me many times. Let us deal with this first. It is more important. Did you eat something out of the ordinary?"

Johnson looked at him as if to say, *How stupid do you believe me to be?*

"All right, then," Edwards continued. "I'm going to give you what is called a purgative, which will force out what is left inside you. I warn you; I may do this a few times until I see the blue tint leave your lips."

Johnson nodded stoically. He gestured for Edwards to lean in. When the doctor did, Johnson spewed the words intensely into his ear. "If I go…the letter. Burn it. Do you understand? *Burn it!*"

Sarah's eyes widened a bit, but she said nothing. Edwards nodded, drew the stiff rubber tube from his bag, and took a deep breath before he began to shove the tube down Johnson's wide mouth.

Sarah, her skirts and apron drenched with dark vomit, carried what she hoped would be the last of Johnson's emissions from the room. It was near dawn. She had held Johnson's shoulders down as his stone-hard body rocked upward each time Edwards purged him. Sarah was more than five years younger than Mr. Johnson, but he was easily twice as strong. She had bruises on her arms now, and her head throbbed mercilessly.

She stopped when she heard Isabel coughing, and then saw her standing at the other end of the hall. She saw just the girl's bare feet sticking out below her nightdress. When she walked closer, she saw

Isabel's tiny body wedged tightly inside the last doorway, where the door met the stair wall. So tight she was that the cornice moldings held her fast; Isabel could not have sunk to the floor had she wanted to.

"What are you doing up, child?" Sarah asked sternly. She was all roles to Isabel: moral guide, seamstress, nursemaid, cook. Yet she stopped short of any true emotion. Not because she did not want to offer the child love—she had attached to her the moment she had seen her a few years ago—but because she was sure Isabel would not accept it. Isabel was a child with too clear a heart. So discipline came easier this way, for both of them.

"Is he dead?" Isabel asked softly...hopefully.

Sarah stood a moment, walked up to her, and without missing a beat, slapped her hard across the cheek and then she said, "I have seen your feeling rising up in you these past few years, child. He was cruel to bring you here. I know. But you can't do anything like this again. Do you hear me? NEVER AGAIN!"

Isabel darted her eyes quickly. She wasn't sure how Sarah could have figured out what happened, and she needed time to find words. Sarah grabbed Isabel's thin fingers and saw the touch of white dust on the tips.

"If he knew—"

"He's an efrit. A devil!" Isabel's voice barely rose above a whisper.

"—he would kill you, child. Do you understand me? Have you forgotten the pictures of hell I showed you? Is that what you want? That's where real efrits live. And that's where you'd end up." Isabel believed her.

Sarah touched the place where she had slapped with her fingers. Then she began the descent down the stairs. "Georgia has warm parritch on the stove, and she will put some calendula on the raised cheek."

Isabel waited a moment, staring at the door, and then let go of the anger. Several tears slipped down her cheeks and swirled around her neck. She followed Sarah down the wide stairs.

CHAPTER
TWO

The Northern Atlantic brings so much to shore. All oceans offer this. The South China Sea brings up a delightfully strange array of surprises, spilling old memories against the sea walls of the mainland. The North Sea regurgitates its oft-foul past and throws it atop the stone caves in Scotland.

The Atlantic is different, only in that it protects its hidden secrets better than most. Its frigid waters are a preservative. In early spring, the waves pull what is underneath—buried in its opaque gray folds, iced solid often—and deposit the forgotten gifts on the eastern shores. Random, anonymous items scatter along the cold sand, cold as brick or frozen brown sugar. Once the sleet and icy floes melt away, the sand begins to soften, and what lies inside its layers emerges.

Rings have been found, carried from ships that had fallen somewhere between the northeastern coastline and Barbados or Jamaica. The rings bear old coats of arms, but also the mystical symbols of castaways or renegades who fled one life in desperate chance they would catch a new one whole. There are footstools, vanity mirrors, shoes, and saddles. There are crates that wash up, wine bottles roiled but snug on the inside, coffee and tools, seed pods, spoiled sewing patterns, vases, window frames, cases of watered-down whiskey, and, of course, *guns*.

1890

Joseph Johnson let his horse linger behind his father's. He wanted to have a chance at second glances, to get to know his father… really, his face. Joseph knew nothing about his father, save for what he would write in letters. When they met at the port in New York, he saw nothing that could offer him clues, either. Samuel Johnson's eyes were narrow, and little light entered, so Joseph could hardly tell when speaking to his father whether he had been heard properly. Samuel Johnson's tone was maddeningly even, with no cadence or rhythm—no notes, as his mother would say. The heart gave off its expressions via the voice, she believed. But Samuel Johnson, he was a guise. His gait, his laugh when it happened, his orders…they all seemed the same to Joseph. He had come a long way to see his father, and now he wanted what he deserved: a good look. A way in. But with Samuel Johnson, there seemed to be none.

His father stood ramrod-straight atop his horse. His gaze circled evenly, from the whitecaps to their left and then over to the orchards and farmland that lay across low, sloping hills to their right. Joseph could see small hints of himself in his father's looks. They were nearly the same height; Joseph had an inch or so on him but not much more. They were both well-built men and their coloring matched, even though Joseph was wind-burned and salt-grazed from the journey over.

His voice, though—there, they were utterly different people. Joseph wondered a few times whether this was just his age; he would turn twenty in a few days, so maybe his voice had not dropped fully. Samuel's was filled with gravel, as if he smoked incessantly or rolled stones down his gullet, but from what Joseph could tell, this was not true. There was something else, something unreal about Samuel's voice. "Un-lifelike" was what first came to mind. But then Joseph erased that thought as quickly as it had arrived.

"I didn't know what to expect before I came," Joseph said. "You read so much about America. And yet it is all in your head."

"Is it what you imagined?" his father asked.

"It feels…endless. I can see for miles in any direction."

His father stood higher up on the saddle. "So, yes: The property lines, they began, as I said, ten miles back. Not endless, but almost. Then it is Johnson land that way, north, northwest, for about six and one-quarter miles. From the south, Johnson land begins just beyond the ironworks."

"May I ride further? Such a day to be out and about. The property, it's more than I had expected."

"Yes. Guests arrive midday tomorrow, Joseph. The wine cases need counting and corking beforehand. That can be done before supper, though. You will need a pressed suit for tomorrow. Are you…?"

"Fitted out? Yes, Father. I did as you asked, and London suited me with four or five suits."

"All right, then," Samuel said evenly.

They waved and parted. Joseph kicked his horse into a high gait and let her speed, and then speed some more, as they veered toward the soft sands along the beach.

He was infatuated already. The air was clean, the gentle noises, the waves and the wind, the gulls…it was nothing like noisy, sooty London. The land, the carving of solid earth from what had been grasslands into mannered orchards, long, sweeping black roads that divided the rich tree groves…it was both graceful and formidable. His own, strange father had done this; it was making Joseph's heart beat fast. He galloped along, his face turned up once to laugh, and the tears the winds made dried off his cheeks before he could touch them.

He slowed a mile or so later, several hundred yards before a small cabin that stood at the end of the dunes. He could see only the stone roof at first, but then, as he urged the horse up off the shoreline, he saw the flat stone that made up a two-room cabin. He leaned into the horse's neck as the large animal's muscles recoiled, then fired. The animal punched and stretched as it launched its front legs up the dune and off the beach.

When he looked back, what he saw…or felt…he wasn't quite sure; it was too sudden. A wind took his hat, his hair, his coat sailed high into the air, flapping against the back of his neck, and with it he saw…what? The wash of an image, a watercolor, a soft, hazy image…slender, bare arms, thick, ebony hair that fell carelessly across her shoulders, olive skin that darkened as the sloping muscle that wrapped her ribs fell. The ribs, as she twisted, caged loose, revealing quick hints of bare breasts.

The wind was playing devilish tricks on him, surely. He brushed his hair from his eyes and leaned down to catch his hat in the horse's tangled mane. Then he looked up again. The girl—now a woman—was tall enough, with the long, somewhat awkward legs of a colt; she could be no more than eighteen. Her long neck stretched as she walked past cotton sheets dancing atop a clothesline. She did nothing to help tame them; they blew high and low as the winds shifted mischievously. Instead, she rotated in a circle. She was, indeed, bare from the waist up: the sheets outlined her breasts and shoulders once or twice. She stopped and let her arms rise to the sky, pulling them out of their sockets. When the sheets dipped, he could catch a small glimpse of her; she allowed her face to soak in the sun, her eyes closed.

He did not move, or even breathe. The horse shifted its balance once or twice, but he barely noticed. He was about to move off the horse, not thinking what a man's presence might do to her. But then she bent down, picked up a blood-hued madras shawl tangled amid some stones, and wrapped it closely around her. Joseph panicked. He was sure if she saw him she would be frightened, angry, or both. He stupidly pushed the horse backward, which made the animal balk, and its back hooves slipped carelessly down the dune, throwing them both dangerously off balance.

"Come on!" Joseph urged, tension in his voice.

He rubbed the horse's backside and it understood, snorting anxiously until it could transfer weight, wrench its body, and slide down the dune face-forward. Joseph stopped only when he thought the horse was safe. He could see nothing now above the steep dune save for the young woman's hands and the shawl. Her arms were outstretched to their fullest, holding the shawl—used as a kite, or a sail, maybe—above her. Maybe the copper-colored arms that lay below were open to the warm winds that swirled everywhere. But he was too far away at this point to know for certain.

CHAPTER THREE

The waltz the small orchestra began to play in the Johnsons' ballroom—the best room in the house, without question—did not begin large. It was music meant to slip into the heads of everyone slowly, seductively. It did not kick-start the way many waltzes did; it started the way a small ensemble piece does, with tiny sounds—adorable, excitable sounds that ran about the floor of the open dancing hall like mice. The sounds whirled around the ankles of the girls, making them giggle. Some grew restless and let their small hands graze their escort's arm. Others, the most flirtatious ones, would lean in and allow the soft curls that had escaped the pins in their hair to fall across their escort's cheek, or maybe even their chest.

It was a signal—a buoyant, lovely signal that the music would rise, and with that, they would begin dancing—or, the way the girls saw it, a moving embrace. There were few moments in life when men and women could remain locked in each other's arms, be it in the bedchamber or, even more wantonly, in a large room filled with the cousins and aunts, the city officials, the dandied-up ironworks foremen. The idea of a long, sanctioned hug, a moving hug, was irresistible.

To the more seasoned women, the women who knew what it was to love, it was a siren's call.

To the beginners—the ones who did not know how a long embrace could feel, in both the wrong and right hands—the waltz drew the fears out of them as nothing else could. These girls fidgeted with their skirts and darted their attentions to everything and nothing. But both the experts and the amateurs responded in one similar way: they felt the sounds that came from the orchestra; it sank into all of them. Every one of them all began, either a little or a lot, to sway.

Sarah, in her stiffest formal service dress, moved about the ballroom with complete precision. She would stop and smile broadly here and there, her political judgment at work, knowing to whom to curtsy, say a kind word or offer a compliment, and where a small smile and nod would suffice. Once she left the hall and was inside the foyer, where staff were positioned to help guests liberate themselves from cloaks or muddied boots, then her feet gained speed as she ascended the wide stairs to the second floor.

She picked up skirts and hurried along the hall, worrying over vases with fresh flowers placed along the corridor, examining the deep rug that led the length of the hall, looking for signs that it had been swept properly the day before. She paused at Mr. Johnson's wide bedroom door and tapped her knuckles twice. She had been head of staff for so many years that her daily life was filled with various codes: the number of looks she gave the cook if the parritch was not thick enough to eat, the degree to which her voice went gruff and tense when the cows hadn't been milked enough, the number of raps she made on the master's door so he knew just who was on the other side.

"Come in, Sarah," she heard him say.

She swung the door open as Mr. Johnson stood before his mirror. He was exceptionally strong, his shoulders wide, his torso hard with muscle. His eyes were slate-gray, his chin cut from stone. He looked like solid rock—save for a lined scar that ran from cheek-bone to jaw. He was almost ready. His shoes were still to the side, though polished to a shine; his shirt was on, and he was attending to the tie his valet had laid out earlier. His hair, as always, was matted to his head. Sarah had never once seen his hair fly about—it was wet and dull gray.

"I'm on my way," he said.

Sarah's brow wrinkled with nerves. "The Ermans have indeed come."

"I thought you said—?"

"Yes. Yes, that's what their message was this morning. Now it seems they are here. I checked just now. There was no further message from them. We are full up on place settings, if you remember—the Eslingtons brought their cousins, and Tillivers are four, not two. So I've had the Ermans, with your approval, fitted into the middle supper tables…" She paused to see if this was a plan.

"They are careless people," said Mr. Johnson. "Who lets them think they can afford to be? Yes, that's fine. We are uncorked properly?"

"Yes, sir. Eighteen cases right now, which Joseph thought would be more than enough. He's readied several more, though, in case he's wrong."

Joseph had hoped to meet as many people as possible over the course of the evening. This was his father's world all gathered at once, the foremen and managers of the ironworks factories. Friends from as far away as Durham and Chicago had accepted invitations, and Joseph truly wanted to know them all.

He had brought his father to life by force, making up lies and half-truths in the years he had grown from boy to man as it had suited him, or as his imagination had allowed. Samuel Johnson, for Joseph, was a drawn illustration. That was why Joseph learned to use his fists. Boys in school, when they met along the Heath—the wild park that ringed Hampstead—had so many places to stage all-day games without the interference of adults, where the boys could push each other recklessly, a favorite pastime at age ten, eleven, twelve...broken noses, collarbones, deep bruises, cuts, scrapes, all were part of the daily games. The boys went home proudly sporting their injuries as badges of honor that determined who was head of the pack. Joseph, like all of the other boys, was offered strange dares to prove himself. Questions that put him on the spot included:

> "How does your family treat the servants?"

> "Whom has your father sired?"

> "Would you hit a master if you could?"

> "What goes on in your trousers when girls walk by?"

There were vicious tell-all games, testing and taunting, egging each other to stand up and be counted, yell the loudest, jump the farthest, swim the deepest. Each day someone new would up the stakes. Joseph used these moments to create a father who exceeded all of their expectations, a mythical god. Joseph created a Samuel Johnson who was everything to everyone: a man who strangled a viper on his travels to India. (Joseph had no idea whether his father had even been to the Raj, but from his letters, he seemed to be a man who would attract adventure.) He was a man of uncommon genius, a man who killed for what he believed in. Joseph told them his father had been in the House of Lords longer than the fathers of any of the other boys in school. Those arguments, about power and pedigree, always, always resulted in shouting matches, kicks, and teeth bashing. He also created a man who was a player in history. He told his friends stories about his father taking iron pipes to President Benjamin Harrison. A boy twice his size sat and listened to this story quietly, and then stood up and called him a liar to his face.

That evening, his nurse sat on the edge of his bed. She didn't say much, applying salve to the bruises he had received from merciless pounding against a stone wall at Hampstead Hill. Joseph wouldn't admit it, but he was relieved. He had begun to hate the stories by that point, and the fight was a rage that felt…liberating.

"Why tell them lies?" his nurse asked him after a long spell.

"How do you know they're lies? He sends letters to me, not you."

He had started to think about how to force his mother to tell him real stories. But she disappeared before he was old enough to press her, the year his father first came to see him in person. "The past is the past," was all his nurse would say after she had gone. "If you let it use you, you will drown."

It easily could make him insane, the blank spaces. And now, now that he had his father in front of him, he was scared off—he asked very few questions. Samuel Johnson was forbidding, deadly silent, and sharply threatening. Now here he was, immersed in the stories that would fill the cracks, the dark holes that left Joseph lost. He was sure the stories and the pictures and the man would cure him of his doubts. He was sure of it.

Joseph had been engaged by guests from the moment he entered the room. Families would introduce themselves; girls would come and ask him too many questions, and the men, they all talked money. He searched the room when he was given a chance. The girl, Elizabeth, the one he waited for, what all this fuss was about, was described to him in vague detail—first by his father, who told him nothing in the end, then by the kitchen staff, who acted like a bunch of geese, pecking at him with jokes, peppering their stories of Elizabeth with pinches to his cheeks and ribs. He wanted to see for himself finally: Was she as delicate as they said?

She was pale and blonde…small-boned, and quiet…a soft voice, which you had to lean in to understand.

His eyes roamed the room for a match. He stood at the party's edge, along the light beams that came off the upper branches of the trees ringing the house. The light beams arced and moaned in the wind. It was an especially windy day, and dancing leaves looked like bird flocks. Joseph stopped as he saw a pair of arms wrapped partly around a tree trunk that stood in the outer circle. He knew them, those slender arms, brown like pennies, the fingers probing the bark. He stepped closer to the window and watched, waiting for her to lean in. *Step out…he said silently to himself. I want to see you… Come out, so I can see…I want—I want—*

…And then she did as he asked. Her cheeks glued to the trunk, she leaned forward…she let her eyes narrow suspiciously at the carriage that came drifting toward the front door. He could see how intent she looked, how she watched the guests alight, the details of the dress, from hem upward to the waist and bust. Her eyes were pointed, deep, and angry—a blue that made him step back slightly. He felt his hand shake the smallest amount.

"Have you seen her?"

Joseph jumped slightly. He turned to find Sarah standing behind him.

"Sarah…no, no, not yet. Is Elizabeth here?" He turned back to the window; the girl was gone.

"I don't see her yet, either. You will know her, though. I can promise you that."

"She is beautiful, I suspect you mean?"

"Yes, of course. And poised."

"What more?"

"What more do you need?"

"Yes. It's a start, right?" Joseph leaned in, teasing Sarah.

"If I were to tell you the things that matter, then the mysteries of the day would be gone." She leaned in conspiratorially now, too. "Look for the most beautiful green gown."

Joseph did as he was asked, but then he slowly let his eyes drift back out through the window. He could hear his father speaking in his peculiar monotone voice, asking about guests, inquiring after children's health. Samuel offered his hand to a woman named Lady Rose, telling her as he led her into a dance that his son would wait to dance the first dance with Elizabeth Edwards. "It's only right," Joseph heard him say. They were engaged, after all, and that was the sole reason for the party in the first place. Otherwise, the evening could be spent doing something productive.

The soft hush of chiffon filled Elizabeth's ears. She had trouble hearing the music as it sailed past her. She kept her eyes lowered, worried that her dress was not hanging properly; that the women would talk first of that. She felt frail, more so than usual; too many eyes were on her. She hated the white light—it made her lose her words. She was a practiced young woman who knew social graces better than most, spoke two languages perfectly, played cards and read extensively…and was a very good conversationalist. But that was only at home where she felt herself. Her father always overlooked what she could do and focused mostly on what she couldn't do. He often told friends that what she lacked in intelligence she made up for in instinct—a trait he expected in women. As Elizabeth found that most others felt this same way, she acted accordingly.

The strands of hair slipped across her eyes, blinding her for a second. She had held her breath, for the dress had slipped between her stockings and the chiffon felt dangerous. She stopped suddenly as she gripped her waist and told herself to breathe. "Nerves," she said quietly to herself. "This is pure nerves." She dabbed the sweat that had formed above her lip, readjusted her curls, and stepped inside the ballroom.

She was several paces ahead of her parents. She knew she should wait to be seen with them but she had no patience, nor any endurance. The one daguerreotype she had been shown of Joseph led her to think he looked something like his father, and she hoped against hope this wasn't altogether true. Samuel Johnson scared her half to death, as he did most people. He was imposing, and lacked the magnetic draw that could make threat attractive. But the photo tint she saw when she looked a second, third, and fourth time hinted at something else, a soft...searching in the young Joseph's eyes. Maybe a curiosity for the unknown, maybe even a sense of abandon. It was...intriguing at first, and then, as her imagination grew, it became a way to see him, a way to begin. She had waited weeks and weeks to see for herself, to see if the yearning eyes meant what she hoped. So where was he? Why could she not spot him instantly in the room, if he was as tall as everyone said, if his eyes were that green—

"I knew I'd spy you first."

She jumped, bumping the back of her head against Joseph's cheek. "Ow!" and "Oh!" collided between them. She spun back and saw Joseph clutching his hand to his eye.

"You have an effective right hook," he said. "Good to know."

Her face bloomed red. She tried to smile, which helped, because she melted men this way, and her hand went up to meet his face. "Oh, forgive me. I am so—"

Joseph captured her hand quickly and gripped it protectively so she paused, losing her breath for a second before continuing, "—cold. Your hands, they need to be warmed. Lucky I came around when I did." She let her hand rest inside his for as long as he wanted. "Joseph—" was all she could get out of her mouth.

He smiled ear to ear and nodded happily. "I've been waiting—"

"Me too," she said, without thinking. "For too long, it feels like."

He looked at her closely now. His eyes turned up in approval at what he saw. They proceeded by her grazed cheeks, then her neck, down along the scooped pearl-like bodice, and past her waist. "I should have taken a faster boat, shouldn't I?" he said, making her blush again. "Stupid mistake."

"How did you know it was me?"

"Honestly?" He whispered this so she could only nod; she had forgotten her words again. "You were pointed out to me the moment you entered the front door," he continued. "I am not a magician…unfortunately."

She nodded again. "I was coming first to look for you. Promise."

"Ahh, good, I like an honest woman," he said lightly. "You are shaking, Elizabeth. Are you all right?"

"Yes, just nervous. Aren't you?"

"Yes. I hide it better is all. But we shouldn't be, should we? We are half family already. Our fathers have been the best of friends for years."

"Sarah has fed you round, romantic tales, I can see." She laughed a bit as she felt the room. Eyes were beginning to turn their way toward her.

"Are they not friends?" Joseph asked. "All the letters my father sent me led me to think—"

"Is it the loveliest night for a party, or not?" She moved closer, into his waist, and said the words just for him. Her perfume was so light, hints of jasmine hit his nose, and he felt slightly off balance.

"It is. Would you like to dance? With me, I mean."

His look sent her sailing; she was sure he said, "With me— only me….*Only* me." It was not true, but she seared it in the memory of the evening until it became a fact.

"Yes," she said softly. "I have been practicing at home a long time."

He slipped his hand behind her and let it rest gently on the small of her back. He began to use his feet—tentatively, at first—

but she was stiff. He was grateful for that; otherwise, he would land on her toes quickly, awkwardly.

"What did you mean just then about our fathers?" he asked after a silent circle about the floor. A few young men his age gave him the once-over, and more than a few eyed Elizabeth. They were a handsome couple, easy to look at, comfortable and harmonious—pretty children were easy to picture. Elizabeth felt as if her life were an egg and the shell had just begun to crack.

"I am all feathers tonight," Joseph said. "I have no idea what I'm talking about. Don't listen to a word I say. Truly." He laughed. She was a good dancer—practiced, very artful, neither instinctive at movement nor naturally able to feel her feet on the floor, but still sweet and very easy to lead. "Would you like some champagne after this?" he asked her. "I was uncorking bottle after bottle this afternoon. It can't go to waste, you know—champagne has no half-life."

"I don't even need a drink." She looked at him, her guileless eyes open and clear. He thought to touch her hand briefly, but it was too late. The music had stopped, and the guests had begun to drift back to the outlines of the room where they would talk, gossip, and laugh until the sun told them to eat. The rituals were never demanding, nor were there ever surprises. They met, they gathered, and then they left each other just as they had found each other—unchanged, unruffled, unexamined.

CHAPTER FOUR

Olive was wrestling the cotton sheets onto the line when she spied Joseph leaning against the tree nearest her. She paused. It was far too early for him to be awake. She smiled, wondering if he had not yet gone to bed.

"Morning, Master Johnson," she said. "Beautiful day, isn't it? Excitable, the winds are, but we love that here. Only thing it's not good for is hanging the laundry. I've been known to chase sheets clear into the orchards on days like this one."

"Hullo, Olive," he responded warmly.

"I saw you dancing last night with Miss Elizabeth. We all did. You looked like two pigs in a poke, Sarah said. I would have to agree."

"She does dance well. She smells like powdered sugar." He smiled, knowing he would make Olive blush, but he didn't much care.

"You should be sleeping in. Last of the free days and all…"

He nodded, but didn't have much of an answer. "I haven't yet met the early morning staff, here or at the ironworks."

"Right. You met the baker, Charles, on your way out here, then? He's the first up in the house. He's been with Mr. Johnson almost as long as Sarah. The two liveries, they're around somewhere. I saw them when I first started today—twins, the only ones in the county, Ben and Missoni. Italian. They take Mr. Johnson out in the coach when he needs it."

Joseph smiled and nodded. After a pause, he said, "The girl down the shoreline, in the stone cabin…I have not met her formally…."

He waited for her to answer. When she didn't, he got up and moved closer. He found her behind a large bedsheet, pinning it securely to the line. His face still held the question and he waited some more.

"Isabel, you mean?" she asked innocently, darting her eyes a bit.

"Is that her name? She lives in the cabin—"

Olive glanced quickly toward the main house and then into Joseph's eyes, trying to see if she could find a foothold. "Yes. She's in the cabin full-time now…poor thing."

"Did she live up here once?"

"Aye, for most of her life, since she was this high." She cut her hand across the top of her knees. "A wee thing she was when she arrived here."

"Is she part of the staff? Did she—?"

"The work staff? No. Did all the chores the way we all do, but no, not formal-like…." She began to feel as if she had already said too much and she moved away from him. "I may have to bolt down the line today. If it springs free and the sheets go flying into the orchard during harvest, I'll just be starting my workday all over again."

He followed her as she zigged and zagged her way through the various clotheslines. "How did she come to live here?"

She did not answer him. "Olive?" He sounded more insistent than he liked.

She stopped and turned, her nerves getting the better of her. "Maybe you should talk to Sarah about her. It's not my place to be saying these things, Master Johnson."

He did not stop her from moving away from him, but he did say, "You can trust me, Olive. I don't talk. Ever. I learned that early on."

She looked back and sighed. "She has the chest illness. Tuber—Tuberc—"

"Tuberculosis?"

"Yes. The terrible one. Dr. Edwards told her over the winter. Six months they gave her, they say. So young. It started off like a normal fever, but she was crying in pain, and they sent for Dr. Edwards one night, and he told Mr. Johnson straight away to get her out of the house. I've got two small ones at home. And the twins, they have their elderly mother and a baby cousin to feed."

"Yes. No. Of course. It was the only thing to do. Why did she live here in the first place?"

"You don't know?" Olive asked openly.

"No. I don't. Should I?"

"Mr. Johnson, he found her drowning in the sea long south of here on one of his exotic travels. He saved the girl and brought her on the boat and has taken care of her since."

Joseph nodded again. He felt agitated now, unable to sit still or think in a silent, logical way. He wanted to know more, but he was sure he had pushed the conversation as far as it would go. Tuberculosis? It was a terrible disease. He had seen it twice, in the span of a few days, near Southampton, before his ship set sail for America. It ate away at the body in short order. The victims he saw were skin and bones, their arms and legs brittle sticks, barely able to bend.

Isabel. Why didn't he ask her last name as well? She was browned by the sun; soft, well-fed curves, the face, a round moon face that was open…fierce…so striking and alive. He shut down the thoughts, forcing them out of his head, away from where he could sift through them. She was sick. She would be gone before he could even begin to know who she was. He told himself to let it go—now. For if he let the thoughts he had invited in to take hold… well, that would not be smart for anyone concerned.

CHAPTER FIVE

Sarah had almost finished packing a basket. It was brimming over with balls of yarn, needles for knitting, fresh berries from the blackberry bushes outside, jam, vinegar, fruit oils, and a few books. Some were about history, but others were romance novels—those, she tucked into the bottom. Atop it all was a freshly plucked chicken wrapped in bacon.

She slipped a thick cotton apron around the top of the basket, fastened it at the sides, and secured her best walking shoes. The walk down the shore took at least half an hour. Last, she looked for her shawl. She was about to slip out the back kitchen door when she felt a hand—it felt more like a claw fastened against her bones.

She paused to find Samuel Johnson standing behind her, his eyes glued to the basket at her feet. "Are you on your way out, Sarah?" he asked, too softly for her comfort.

"Good morning. Yes. Have you had your breakfast?" She shifted her weight back and forth once too often.

"Yes. Where are you going with that?"

"It's just a bit of cake from last night. A book or two to pass the time…I thought…" Her words died suddenly.

"You thought what, Sarah?"

"I thought I'd take the basket down to the cabin."

"No."

"She has no one—"

"No."

"Sir—"

"It's not safe. I've told you that. Clearly. I was sure I didn't need to repeat myself. I never do with you...or do I?"

She looked down at the basket. She felt hot tears come to her eyes, but she would not allow Mr. Johnson to see them, so she bent down and wiped her cheeks with her apron with a quick swipe. "I was not going to put myself at risk. I would leave the basket outside the front door. She needs things, sir. She can't—"

"Didn't you hear me? You won't go down there."

"Yes, sir. I understand." She picked up the basket and placed it next to the kitchen hearth. She took the bushel of berries, thinking she needed a rigorous task now, something that would keep her from weeping. She would boil them down for their sugars.

"Sarah?"

She turned so slowly, for reasons that must have confused her. She had worked for the man for more than twenty years and was not easily shaken in general. But right now, he frightened her. What she might see forced her eyes to the floor before they rose. When she met his gaze, his was so...stony. He was never a man to reveal himself, but here now, it was as if he had no breath inside him.

"Joseph is not in his room. Do you know where he is?" She let out a breath; relief filled her chest. Such an innocuous question—what made her shiver so?

"No, sir. I haven't seen him yet this morning." Then she grabbed the bushel of blackberries and made her way to where the sugar vats waited. "Don't let your breakfast get cold, sir." She had regained the strength in her voice, her command of all faculties. She was grateful for that.

"Have Ben take the basket down to the cabin." She nodded in response without looking up.

Samuel Johnson felt his coffee go down cold. His insides never felt much; he needed hot peppers, chilies, and red powders, like the ones used in stews and roasts in the Caribbean, to feel as if a meal had hit his stomach. The rest of the time he made do by chewing and swallowing. He glanced at his watch once too often. He thought to abandon his meal altogether and look for Joseph, but he decided to sit still. His son could be anywhere.

The young man he had met at the docks in New York surprised him. Joseph had changed since his father had last seen him. Now Joseph was looser; funnier, certainly. Samuel had watched him entertain several guests and reduce them all into giggles faster than anyone he had ever seen. Yes, his son had a quick mind now, and did not need to be told anything twice.

Samuel also observed how curious Joseph had become. Samuel remembered a child in London who was spindly, introverted, and pliable; he had been that way at his age, too, but there was a distinction: he wanted always, every day, to find a path forward. His ambitions were first and foremost. He saw people as either hindrances or gateways; he had little interest in them otherwise. Joseph now had an interest in people that was, he guessed, without agenda. Innocent emotions like that worried Samuel— they weren't the makings of a lion.

Joseph appeared a moment later. He had the bloom of a long walk on his cheeks. His hair went every which way; the tips of his ears shone bright red. "Good morning."

"And to you." Samuel poured coffee for his son. "I lost track of you last night."

"I was here all evening. I saw you take the stairs to bed about midnight."

"When did Elizabeth and her parents leave?"

"I walked them to their carriage shortly after you retired."

"Have you been out already? It's early."

"I wanted to meet the staff. I like Ben—he and his livery twin are rascals. I can make friends with them easily." He smiled.

"And Olive," Samuel added.

"Yes, Olive. Very sweet."

They sat in silence through half the meal. Joseph really didn't feel like talking, and it irritated Samuel. "You haven't said anything about Elizabeth," he said.

"She's lovely. Who is the girl down the beach, Father?"

Samuel began to check his mail as he made to stand and leave for the day. He refused to look up; his attentions had shifted elsewhere. "Isabel—" was all he said. Joseph waited, but his father said nothing more than the one word.

"And? Tell me about her. I understand she is ill?"

"Yes, very," Samuel answered crisply.

"I heard she lived here before that. In this house? That she has been here since she was a child—I mean, she is down there alone. Who cares for her now?"

"I do." He looked up, dropping his mail on the thick wooden table. "I do…as I do everyone else here. You included."

Joseph felt his heart beating faster, but he had no idea why. "What did she do here? She seems so—"

"You have met her?" Samuel's gaze was pointed, accusing.

"No—I just saw her a day or so ago—from afar. I wonder how she could have caught such a terrible condition. No one else here is infected, are they? I mean, is there nothing that can be done?"

"Joseph, you are irritating me to no end. What are you? A child? Is this how you want to start the day? With useless diatribes on injustice?"

"No—I—"

Samuel continued as if he didn't even hear his son. "I don't start forest fires with my teeth, and I am not the apocalypse, able to give birth to deadly disease per my will. So can we talk about something else, please?"

Joseph sat back in his chair. He did sound feeble—stupidly so. He also felt six years old, angry over the world's injustices. He wasn't a child, and he hated thinking his father saw him as one. "Just…tell me how she came to be here."

Samuel looked up. His eyes turned the palest gray, the color blending with the whites of his eyes, making him seem like a wolf. "When I left Colombia for my return to New York, we'd been sailing a few hours when a storm struck. We came across a small boat. We did what we could to get to it, but we were too late. We found Isabel holding onto what was left of the bow…the mother and the others aboard had perished." He took in some coffee. "We turned about—I hired men to search for other family, but…I decided it best to bring her back here and give her a home."

"She is your adopted daughter?"

"Yes. I don't want you near her, do you understand me? Tuberculosis is highly contagious."

Joseph nodded. "Yes. I understand." He wanted to, at least. That he was sure of; his father's puzzles were more important to him. Much more.

CHAPTER SIX

Joseph sank into the soft cushions in the Edwards' sitting room. It was small, fit for three or four and no more. The large, framed windows, which went from ceiling to floor, flooded the room with light and made the place feel like an expensive dollhouse. It was a warm home. The servants had big smiles; they were small-talkers and got Joseph to rattle on about the party almost instantly. They left him in the sitting room with hot coffee and warm biscuits and yelled the way cousins might shout for Elizabeth to come downstairs and talk with her important beau.

He kneaded the cup, restless, not in the best of moods, but unable to sort out exactly why. When Elizabeth appeared, saying just "Hullo" to his low "Hullo," she was dressed in a soft linen gown. It made her look fragile and sweet. He chastised himself for being wrapped up in himself and then he stood, happy to let her distract him.

"The custard fell," she said as she sat down across from him. She actually looked as if she might cry. He gestured for her to sit nearer and she shyly accepted.

"Sorry? Repeat what you just said."

"I wanted to make you a mousse, to go with your tea. Custard, I think you call it in England."

"A soufflé?"

"Yes, yes, that's the name. And we put it in the icebox to chill, and sometime during the afternoon, it collapsed."

He watched her in silence, her lips a thin line. She waited for him to respond, and he would take her cue from there. She rarely offered up her own feelings without someone in the room acting as leader. When his eyes turned and he laughed, she let out a small breath of air. Her mouth curled into a smile and she let out a giggle. "Sorry," she said happily.

"It's all right," he replied, letting his arm slide across the back of the sofa behind her. "I'll live."

He launched into a series of stories, each one funnier than the last, about his London cook's adventures in the kitchen. She was an utter failure in the kitchen—a fact everyone ignored. And her bravado in spite of it all, attempting dishes that made the most courageous eater curdle in fear, made her infamous among his friends, who launched her food as footballs after supper. The moment he stopped, he saw her eyes dim, and she slipped back into the somewhat sad state that was usual for her.

"Is something wrong?" he asked after eyeing her carefully.

"No, thank you for asking. I am fine. This is my natural face. Yes, yes; I am well."

He sat back into the couch.

"Our lives are about to change in such profound ways," she continued. "Since last night…you are an excellent conversationalist, by the way."

"Thank you."

"I'm filled with jitters—and questions, I think. Leaving my family. America, gone. London, hullo. Marriage is something I barely understand." She looked at him straight on for the first time. His eyes were intent. He was listening closely to what she said, and it scared her half to death. "I'm sorry. I'm acting like a child."

"No, don't apologize. I'm here to get to know you. Take your time. We can do it slowly…"

"Not too slowly. We're to leave for England in six weeks."

He looked at her and smiled. "I had two powerful reasons to come to America. The first was a beautiful girl named Elizabeth, a girl I was told could set a sail. Those were the words my father wrote me…I don't think he lied about that. The other reason is my father. He is as unfamiliar to me as any person I know. And I wanted that to change."

She liked him, right then in that moment. He was a friend—or could be, at least. He made her chest unravel; the tightness that had existed the past few days released, and she felt her breath lose its spiked inhalations. "I've known your father my whole life. And I don't know him well, either. Very few do." She paused, trusting him suddenly, on instinct. "People say he's an enigma. I visited his house—your house—often, when I was small. I was out and about on the grounds with Isabel. But since we met, I don't even think he has ever looked into my eyes. Isn't that strange?"

"Isabel and you were friends?"

"Are," she answered simply. "I love her."

Joseph leaned in. He wanted to know everything she did now. He wanted to be in her head. But a movement caught his eye, just outside the window, in the garden. It might have been a cat—it moved so swiftly. But then he saw a silhouette—it escaped under the shadows of the large elm that lurched over the house. He didn't have to guess; he knew who it was. It made him sit up straighter. If he could, he would leave, find a story that allowed him into the yard. He placed his cup down on the table and was about to move, but when he looked up, he saw Isabel from the back. She skipped over the fence, out onto the far street, and away.

"Mother says wedding arrangements are often fragile things," Elizabeth mentioned.

"What?" Joseph asked dumbly. "Sorry, sorry. I slipped into a coma for a moment. Yes, they are fragile. It's good that I'm not a meddler."

"It's fine to have your opinions. It's a big day."

"Oh, no—all is fine if it's fine with you. My opinions don't matter."

She laughed, thinking he was being funny again, but she collapsed slightly when she could see he was not looking her way at all. His gaze was far out the window.

Joseph stopped his horse along the beach where the sandy crests collapsed and lost their power. He had promised himself he would take the gravel roads home and avoid this path and the cabin. But he went this way anyway. He wanted to see…what? What exactly was he interested in? Was he morbid? Did he have some twisted need to see how illness unfolded? He'd never felt this way before, drawn to something—or someone—without having one bitter clue as to why.

His father's decision to keep the secret places of his past dark didn't help, of course. Joseph bordered on obsession about who the man was, without new thoughts about this girl—holding the memories just out of his son's reach was an effective form of torture. Joseph thought about idling longer at the Edwards'. He would ask to speak with the doctor, just to see how it might settle his agitation. But instead, he'd left things in an uneasy state with Elizabeth, without knowing why—he also wasn't sure he cared. So he left, quicker than he would have liked, and pushed the horse to make the beach as fast as possible, hoping he might catch her on her way home.

He slipped off the horse and walked up the dune until he was a stone's throw from the cabin door. He was shy, unable to figure out a plan to introduce himself, even though being a Johnson was surely enough reason to say hello. He felt slightly weak, his stomach pitched into his throat, and he closed his eyes to calm himself.

Then he saw her—her slender arms, rising into the wind; that shawl whipping carelessly like a kite. This time she turned and looked his way. She smiled so slowly that he felt the wind knock him backwards. He ran his hand through his hair and felt the sweat form. He wanted to walk toward her…would she even let him? He didn't care. He would do it anyway.

He opened his eyes again and there she stood, in the open doorway of the cabin. Her eyes, unlike the ones in his dreams the past few days, were venomous, brutally angry—they looked intensely black from where he stood. Her hip was cocked against the doorframe, one hand fisted tightly against her leg.

He raised himself onto the horse quickly. He paused, then for a moment, neither of them moved. It happened in one instant— had Joseph turned away or blinked, he would have missed it. But he saw it: her eyes. They looked into his, and when they did, they turned from black to the softest blue. Then she must have felt it, too, for she stiffened, and they went dark again. Her eyes followed his until the last time he looked back. The door was closed, and she had disappeared.

CHAPTER SEVEN

Joseph stopped each time he descended the Johnsons' stairs. A small portrait of his mother hung on the wall by the second-floor landing. She must have been a few years younger than Joseph when she had sat for it. He could barely remember how she looked the last time he saw her, and this portrait was different from what he remembered. Here she was full of possibilities—that's why there was a smile in her eyes, an inner intensity that made her seem... delighted.

What he remembered was a wholly different woman, lost, her compass off-kilter. She had talked in her sleep in the months before she had disappeared, and she had dark circles under her eyes—she seemed haunted. The London house staff had told him she would wake many nights in tears, frightened, shaking, all out of sorts. When they were alone, which was often, Joseph would see a woman who had the most dreadful fears, as if she had spent a life on the run.

This portrait, while chic, was not real, and he knew it. It was maybe why he began to study it every day, like a puzzle piece—one that might help him understand what he was doing here in America.

"Your mother was a handsome woman, Joseph," Sarah said as she passed him going upward.

"Mmm. I saw the carriage leaving. Is Father gone?"

"Yes, sir. 'Problems with the ironworks,' he said. 'Serious,' he said. Employees rising up, refusing to work until he came—something about pipes and how they're fixed proper and improper, and in the proper way, the true amount of time it took to do it all."

"Sarah...which way to find fresh flowers?"

"There are beds about to burst near the southeast orchards."

He set out the door without a meal, without even a good-bye. He couldn't stand to wait even five minutes for Ben to finish shoeing a plough mare. Instead, he went bareback on the horse his father had given him as a welcome present. She was young, attuned to him, and so she did not mind him slipping up, holding her mane and giving her a gentle, firm nudge to escape the barn. The mare nibbled on the lemon grove leaves along the orchard gully while Joseph gathered the early budding tulips. He mixed them with bloodroots and anemones and then slipped onto the mare's back.

He arrived just outside Isabel's door an hour after he had left the main house. He was straining inside his jacket and his chest ached some. He wanted to throw his coat away; his shoulders pulsed so hard inside the sleeves he thought he might break the seams. He let out two, three breaths, then walked to the front door and tapped the wood.

Inside it was silent; silent as a tomb. He stepped to the window and peered inside. It was a sparse house, displaying a table with a single chair. A small kitchen ran along the back, which opened out onto the last of the Johnson property. In her bedroom was a neat pile of linen clothes: blouses, skirts, nothing more. Beyond that were only books, which lined the room so that one could face any wall and use the books lined against the molding as a step-up to touch the ceiling.

He tapped again. Sure that she was not at home—he saw no one sleeping in the single bed at the far end of the second room—he left the flowers at the base of the door. He was about to swing his leg atop the mare when he felt something; a small beat inside his chest and a tug on the back of his neck. He turned to find Isabel standing in the doorframe. A rifle was lodged under her arm. She narrowed both eyes to be sure she hit him square across the body—a dead shot, as they called it—an aim that was meant to kill with one spray of buckshot.

"Oh, wait! No!" he exclaimed, putting up his hands in instant surrender.

"Step back," she ordered.

"Yes. I will—please, though, put the rifle down. You're scaring me to death. My name is Joseph. Joseph Johnson...I'm Samuel's son. I've just arrived...from London..."

"I know who you are."

She did not move a muscle, but he stepped several steps back in any case.

It seemed that she had decided not to shoot him outright, so he said, "I'm here to introduce myself formally. I wanted you to know who I am...I brought the flowers, as a—"

"What are you staring at?" she inquired with suspicious contempt, clearly not having listened to anything he had said.

"What am I—I? You must be joking. It's because you are..." He bowed his head. "I am sorry, I lost my ability to speak for a moment. You are—perfect. It's why I'm staring...I'm not sure, but think I've been blown backwards..." His words drifted off, seeming useless. He let her move as she wished. He let her look at him... every inch.

It was the slowest gaze. It began at his feet and rose slowly up his tensed muscles, across his torso. Then she stopped, and they locked eyes. Neither said a word for the longest time. "You're looking, too." Joseph let a smile appear on his lips, but he stopped when he could see he had just angered her. "At me, I mean. You're as curious about me as I am about you."

"Go away," she said simply.

"Yes, all right." He turned to face the mare. "It's a beautiful day, isn't it?" He decided not to look over his shoulder.

"Did you not hear what I just said?"

"Yes. If you like, I'll leave."

"It's so stupid of you to come here."

"Yes. True." He turned to face her again. "I swear, though, you don't need to be afraid of me."

She laughed. "You are either an idiot or confused; or maybe you hit your head too hard. You have things backward."

"All of the above—at different times." He thought he saw a small break in her gaze and smiled again. She raised the rifle, this time at his face. He lost his humor right after. "You look so…well," he said. "Not sick at all. Do you feel—?"

She pointed the rifle to the sky and took a clear shot upward, which made them both jump. "All right," he said. "I'm clear now. Where did you get the gun, Isabel?"

"Ask your father where he keeps the weapons."

He nodded slowly. "I see." He turned and walked back to the mare. He did not look back this time. He spurred her with his heels coarsely and let her dive down the dune where she wanted to gallop.

Isabel looked at the flowers, inhaled sharply, and slammed the door shut.

Joseph thought about going home, but his head was hot and he needed answers. So he turned toward town, galloped most of the way, and stopped only upon reaching the Edwards' house. He let himself in when no one answered—Elizabeth had told him this was acceptable. He found one of the servants making sun tea in the back.

"Hullo, Millicent. Can I find Dr. Edwards anywhere?"

Millicent gave him a toothy smile and told him to knock on the doctor's office door. "He will answer if he is free," she told him, "and ignore you if he is not."

He did as he was told, and a moment later, Dr. Edwards ushered him toward a sun-drenched chair across from his examining room.

"Have I taken you from something?" Joseph asked before he got comfortable.

"In no way," said the doctor. "The sounds of the house have fallen into a low murmur. I'm going slightly mad. It's taken years to become accustomed to a house filled with women, and now, when they abandon me, I can't seem to do without the hullabaloo."

"Father stole your wife, didn't he?"

"Yes—and Elizabeth. They're in Trenton, to fit out her wedding gown. Final touches, I'm told...*Millicent!*" he yelled through the open door. "Some tea, please!" He turned back to his guest and gestured toward a chair. "Joseph, I mean it. Sit down."

The two sat at once, facing each other. They were silent, awkward, the way two men could easily be at first. "When will they return?" Joseph asked, thinking of nothing better to say.

"This evening, I'm sure."

"Good." He waited for a beat, then said, "I just met Isabel... on my way here."

Edwards nodded, not looking at him directly.

"Did you diagnose her?" Joseph asked. "I mean to say, you *did*. I knew—know that. The house staff told me."

"Yes. She grew up in your father's house. I suppose you know that, too?"

"Yes. What are her symptoms?"

Edwards paused and eyed Joseph a little more closely. "You understand it is a disease of the lungs?"

47

Joseph nodded. "Yes. I've seen tuberculosis patients in England."

"Yes, all right then. It's believed it's caused by bacteria, and while some can go asymptomatic…"

"Without symptoms?"

"Yes. When symptoms do emerge, they start as a terrible cough and then go on to fever, quite a loss of appetite. Well, when the bacteria takes full hold, the blood barriers burst and they begin to cough blood. This is morbid talk for you, isn't it?"

Joseph shook his head a resolute no.

"All right. Anyway, let's talk of livelier things. A young man like you has a long future to hope for."

Joseph smiled, but with no purpose. "And there is no hope for a cure?"

"Oh, no…no."

CHAPTER

EIGHT

Joseph would not consider bed. He had drunk too much at supper; he did it because he thought it would help dull his senses, but instead it just made him pace. He went twice to the stables and opened the door to saddle the mare, and then he forced himself to close the barn doors, once on his own fingers. "Christ!" he yelled loudly to no one.

He had drunk until he felt nothing but darkness enveloping him, but he could not close his eyes. The moment his eyes did shut, she appeared. The strands of her hair caressed his cheeks. Her voice—a soft, hoarse timbre—pierced his ears. He felt hot, then cold, then hot again.

He pulled himself upright when his father arrived. He didn't want to talk to him about this—or anything else, for that matter. He liked his misery better than the reality before him. Within himself, he could sit silently with her, the "her" that was embedded inside him now. It was just the two of them, starkly connected.

"Sarah says you're drunk?" Samuel asked as he came to stand above Joseph, who sat slumped in the wrought-iron chair along the back porch.

"Yes, a bit, I suppose. Not enough, really."

"What does that mean?"

"Nothing. I'm being obnoxious. How did it go? Did you solve the ironworks problems? How is the dress?"

"The dress: rare. Employees: herded—"

Joseph laughed some. "*Herded*, did you just say?"

"As they need to be." Samuel took some of the whiskey out of the decanter and poured himself a snifter.

"What are their demands?" Joseph asked.

"They want—what they can get…the dress. That was the trip, in earnest. The other events were neither here nor there. Is she as beautiful as I said, Joseph?"

"Yes. More than. I do need to know her some, Father, She wants this too, I think."

Ignoring him, Samuel took his son's right hand in his without warning, which made Joseph sit up stiffly. "What is this on your hands?" Samuel asked. "Paint? Have you been painting?"

"Yes, before supper. I do oils." He pulled his hand away. "I used some of the photographs and books you have in your library, from your travels, as inspiration."

Samuel looked back at the orchards. "You haven't said. Will you begin law studies right after your return to England?"

Joseph sat silently—too long, he was sure. His father's gray stare was firmly on him now. "Father, can we not take this more slowly? I barely know Elizabeth."

"Only an idiot feels ready for marriage, Joseph."

"Yes. But I have questions."

"About what?"

"About whether marrying her is the right thing. I want to be sure I feel something for her—and I want to be sure she has no doubts about me…"

"Who does what they want, Joseph?" The silence between them had gone so cold that Joseph was sure his father would walk out. "Honestly. Whoever told you that?"

"You and Mother did not love each other…of course not! Why should I even ask a question like that? I know the answer." He stood. "I'm going to bed, Father. Good night."

But before he could leave, his father took him by the shoulder, grabbing the bone hard. His fingers dug inside the sinews, making Joseph curl backwards. "We were suited, Joseph. Which is what marriage is about." Joseph felt his father's hip lurch again and again. "The thrust, the parry…that's all it is." He let Joseph go. "The rest…that's all pure fiction." Then he left.

"Are you saying no to postponing the wedding?" Joseph called after him.

Samuel was far away when he answered, but Joseph heard him clearly: "Yes, Joseph. That is what I am saying."

Sarah bustled along, her two baskets filled with goods for the cabin. She was spitting nervously. She had waited for Mr. Johnson to leave for New York, and she told herself she had enough time to see to Isabel and get back before supper was needed.

She cut into the dunes when she saw the cabin roof and hurried in as fast as her body would carry her. She slipped inside, feeling safer there. She saw the tulips, half-crushed; they were set inside an empty milk bottle.

"Isabel? Where are you, darlin'? It's me. Where did you get the flowers? They are pretty." She worried over the flowers, truth be told, but decided not to say anything. Instead, she unpacked the goods from the two baskets.

When Isabel appeared from inside the bedroom, she let the girl press her cheek against her own hot skin.

"He is so clever, isn't he?" Isabel said without emotion. "Telling people I'm ill. It was just a very bad cold, Sarah. And he took advantage of the situation."

"I agree with you. It's a big lie, if what you say is true." Sarah took the chicken and placed it by the hearth. "It's been wrapped in goose fat, so it should be delicious."

Isabel took one of the blackberries and popped it into her mouth. Then, without warning, she grabbed Sarah by the shoulders and exhaled into her. Sarah jumped back with such a start it made Isabel laugh.

"Wait. See. Right? If I have what he says, then you'll be sick within days. I'm now going to learn how to play his way." She took another bite and said through her teeth, "If I'm sick, then you're sick."

Sarah's eyes welled with tears. "You have no forethought, do you? Do you truly believe a girl like you—with your history—can be a match for a man like him? Let me tell you a great truth, young thing. The world turns on men's whims. And nothing more."

"Watch me."

"What do you mean?"

"Nothing. Thank you for the basket."

"For goodness' sakes, Isabel! Get ahold of yourself! This life is not half as terrible as you make it out to be. Look outside: the sun is full on. I was half-carried here by bluebirds come nesting for the summer. The blooms are full burst, everywhere. The ocean is singing—"

"That's not the waves, Sarah. It's my mother. She's crying; that's what you hear." "Sometimes she calls me; she begs me to go to her," Isabel said with a broken voice.

Isabel stopped hearing anything Sarah said after that. Now she heard the moans of the water, the way it rocked inward, tearful. Then she heard the ocean, the way it sighed as the undertow pulled the water out, away, and gone.

CHAPTER NINE

Joseph used the late-afternoon light to finish off the painting. He knew who would own it halfway through.

He used some of his father's photographs as inspiration. The photos had been stuffed inside a leather album in the library, tucked behind the year's almanac. Joseph took to one particular photograph more than the others; it offered street scenes from Cartagena. He didn't think he would see the place on his own, but maybe he was wrong. This trip to America had changed him; he was in an inexplicable new place, something he would have never believed possible before. His father—he had all but written him out of his life until the letter that came about Elizabeth, his passage money, and a way forward. *So nothing is written*, he thought.

It whetted his appetite, this picture book. Maybe he would find a way to travel more, not be chained to a desk, gazing at innocuous paper, his face buried in language.

He liked the way the sunlight hit the oils on the canvas. It would have been smart to let it dry properly, but he knew he could not wait for that. He'd hardly had the resolve to leave the cabin that first time, as every other place now seemed *out of place*. He felt tilted, odd, alien...unless he was near her, and he drew plans to fix that. All day he looked for a way back to the cabin, if only so his heart could settle into a proper rhythm. But until then, he was resigned to this state. Now, away from here, he was anything but normal.

The previous night, in the middle of the night, he woke to the scent of lemons. Upon getting close to Isabel that first time, the citrus perfumes rolled along his lips. He touched his bottom lip lightly with his fingers, let out a low growl, and let his head roll back. He did not want to touch himself; his own fingers were doing nothing for him. He had been happy with those types of easy pleasures until this moment. When he had come of age in London, his rowdier friends had introduced him to the pleasures of brothels. He liked the game and learned how to use his hands in bed. The girls had taught him with their soft sounds what felt delicious. But not now. He only wanted…her.

His eyes closed; maybe he could fool himself that way. Maybe he could feel her touch him. It only made his hips torque, so he turned to his side. The soft air suddenly made it seem as if she were lying next to him, her hips curved into him—her hands… *Christ!* He had to stop—these taunts. He took himself with his hand and forced air out of his lungs to get even a few small sips in before losing himself in a shameless climax.

Samuel was up before dawn, and his breakfast was finished shortly thereafter. He would spend the next several days walking the assembly lines at the ironworks. Open rebellions were erupting among the workers; he did not want that virus to spread among the foremen. They were his line of defense, and he ran them with a bullwhip. He wanted all concerned to be sure they understood the cost of opposing him. The stories they had heard about him—were they true? He wanted to walk the lines of workers and have them glance behind their backs so they would be convinced that every story, every word, was worse than they had imagined.

Sarah was clearing Samuel's place as he pulled on his coat. He saw Joseph's boots missing from the vestibule. "Where is Joseph?" His voice was tight and clipped. No one but Mr. Johnson sounded that way.

"I don't know, sir." Sarah paused in her place. "He was not here when I came down. I heard him say he might go for an early walk with Elizabeth, but, as I say—"

"Did you take baskets down to Isabel? As I asked you—told you—not to?"

She stopped again. "Yes, sir. I left early apples at her front step."

His silence told her nothing. She felt a chill run up her spine, and she left the room before he could act.

Isabel began to swim in the ocean a year after she arrived in New Jersey. Sarah, who was much younger then, and who held Isabel's hand so tightly she would squeal, led her into the water. "Stop! You're hurting me!" Isabel would cry. The waves were never ferocious on the days Sarah chose to take her out. She planned it that way, but still, she wanted to be sure the girl could purge her fear of the water. The girl's mother had drowned, after all; Sarah silently believed Isabel must have terrible feelings buried deep inside her. She felt the hair of the dog would cure this. She wanted Isabel to see how beautiful it felt to immerse the body in water. Cold, clean water.

"The soul, every so often, needs a bath," Sarah would say to Isabel as they waded into the low tides.

"What is the soul?" Isabel would ask. She was always curious. She asked a thousand questions a day.

"The soul? It's the part of you that connects your heart and its desires with your head. It can be felt everywhere, the soul; even outside of yourself at times."

She held her tighter, even though Isabel squealed again. "'Oh, God, 'tis a fearful thing / To see the Human soul take wing...' That's Lord Byron for you, Isabel," she would say as she towed into the surf.

Isabel began to swim on her own by the time she was nine or ten. She loved being on her back the most. The waves would kick her around angrily and send her under, forcing her to cough up salt water, but she would just arch her neck and let the sunshine bathe her eyes. She could hear her mother's soft voice when she did this:

> "Do you want me to sing you a song before you sleep? A lullaby? I will..."

> "Hold me tight, Isabel. Feel my arms around you. Always, we will hold each other and be safe this way."

> "Where are you? I miss you, my love...I miss you..."

Isabel emerged from the water and took her hair and twisted it like a cloth mop, squeezing water out onto the sand. She loved early morning swims. She never wore a bathing costume; no one was up early enough to walk the coast in this part of the world, so there was no risk of indecent exposure. It was often cold enough so that, even if a lone soul were to be awake, that person would avoid the chills the surf winds gave off.

Isabel reached for her skirt and blouse and put them on when the sun had burned her skin dry, leaving her with the taste of salt. She stopped briefly before reaching the cabin, noticing an object leaning against the front door. She bent down, eyed it closely, and instantly recognized the street shown in the painting: a crooked path she had walked many times with her mother, leading from their house down to the docks where they would buy spices and fish for supper. She could never have summoned this image herself; it was as if the painting did it for her. She leaned in to touch it, but a male voice made her jump:

"No! Don't, please! The oil paint is still wet."

Her fingers quickly recoiled. "Is this…?"

"Cartagena. At least, that's what I tried to make it look like," Joseph said. "I took it from a photograph in my father's house. It's where you're from, isn't that right? I asked Olive and Sarah."

Isabel stepped back so she could open the door and face him at once. "I'm from Santa Fe de Bogota…and the rifle is in the closet," she said.

He looked relieved. "Ahh," he said as he smiled, which confused her thoroughly. "I want to know you're safe, so it makes me feel good to know it's there." He asked after a moment, "May I possibly come in? I won't overstay my welcome. You can throw me out any time you like."

He waited for her answer. He felt as if he were on a tightrope and a powerful wind had blown through. She finally lifted her eyes and offered her arm, which would allow him to pass her and move inside the cabin. He did not move, though. "I won't come in unless you want me to. I'm not forcing myself on you, Isabel. I'm merely asking you to invite me…to want to, at least see, if I interest you in any way."

When his eyes met hers, he felt a shift. A subtle change lightened her eyes again. He wasn't sure what they were saying, whether the colors reflected fear of him…or curiosity. Maybe it was both.

"I would never hurt you—or any woman, for that matter. It is not in me. You need never be scared of me."

She bowed her head. When she looked at him again, she gestured with her hand, allowing him entry. He let out such a deep sigh, surprising her for the second time in as many minutes. "Thank you," he said and shifted past her, almost too shy to look, and entered the small house.

Cartagena, Colombia, 1880

Samuel Johnson found Cartagena by accident. He had been in Mexico, lingering there for several weeks before moving deeper into the Latin corridor. He visited various Mexican foundries; that was the initial purpose, at least. He had tossed around the idea of how to use the money from his dead wife's estate, and he liked the idea of iron—or maybe ore. But then he stayed longer than he had planned, traveling down the Yucatan Peninsula by carriage and by boat. He would stop for a few days, sometimes longer, take in local sights, eat fresh lobster, drink more than usual. It was blisteringly hot; there was little to do but sleep in the mornings, and he began to like the way he was forced to live in tune with the sun. Soon he emerged into the streets, like most Mexicans, only after night fell.

He learned to distinguish his tequilas, and he picked up enough pidgin Spanish to be able to move about without a translator or a guide. Palapas bars set up along the beaches offered small-boned, highly passive women. They were shy, meek—they even crossed themselves when he got them back to his room and told them what he wanted to do with their bodies. But they did not whimper or cry out once he began. They came to him without his having to do much beyond glancing their way. The young women, they had never seen someone as well-dressed as he before. They were sure he would give them small bills after, or maybe a nugget of gold, grateful for their time. But that never happened.

He moved south after that, traveling through Latin America and into Panama. On his second night in the Colombian city, he was invited to supper. A friend from New York had given him a few names to look up—Americans mostly, but a few British who had repatriated also became drinking companions. Johnson's friend in New York had offered a small hint about why it might be worth his while: "They are pulling off a magnificent coup down there, in Panama. A great, big, man-made canal. Go. Listen."

The canal, the men told Johnson over supper, would be more than…well, just about anything ever tried—the engineering feat of the century. "We are cutting the continent in half," one round American said, his face too red, his saucy eyes popping. "Shipping will cost half as much, goods half as much. Profits…" There the whole table lay silent, then, all at once, they laughed—and hard. "Well. It will change the map," the round man said quietly. Johnson loved the way these men thought. They were big dreamers, unapologetic, rough—rapacious, even. He wondered quietly: *Steel. They will need more!*

He stayed up nights after that making notes, crafting sketches of foundries, writing cables back home inquiring after local properties for sale. The heat had settled in. The talk of malaria, which had wiped out hundreds of the French workers digging the earth, was common at coffeehouses; doctors from as far away as Santa Fe de Bogota and Medellin had been brought in to run a vacant hospital. They all advised him, as they sipped their badly needed espresso, to craft his plans elsewhere. But he had taken to the place. Also, he didn't listen much to others' opinions.

There were signs of death everywhere. It should have silenced Johnson, but he felt nothing but a strange sense of pride. He had money to play with—his wife's estate had seen to that. He was untouched by the sounds of sickness that rang around him. He took women into his hotel who could easily have been sick, but the things he did to them, at night, while the sounds of children's pained cries rang out, were thrilling to him. They made him feel regal.

He heard one night, from a bar owner, about Cartagena. He had begun planning his return home, but he listened as the owner rambled. Cartagena was not just the most beautiful city in Colombia, but "a carnal spot," he said over a brandy. "The Golden Door of South America," he called it later in the night.

Johnson hired a boat a few days after that and landed in Cartagena without a sound. He spent just a few weeks there, eating suppers that stretched into dawn, listening to the sounds of husky-voiced women singing languorous songs, meeting rich men who pushed women and soft liquor into him without ever saying why. The political men were the warmest; they began to charm him into thinking he belonged. It was then he decided he would not wander further, at least not for a year or so. He found a house along La Calle de la Mantilla, bought furniture, and hired a cook the next day.

The narrow elbow on which his two-story Colonial house sat was at the end of a series of crooked streets overlooking the ancient seawall. The street was full of color. Flowery vines climbed the walls of every residence, potted herbs ringed the windowsills, and deep bougainvillea covered the top of every house, linking one home to the next.

The street had no outlet, and the ancient wall dating from the Spanish occupation that surrounded the city silenced even the loudest cries. Whites lived along this street—the women fashionably dressed in graceful linens that hugged them the way sensuous European clothes did. Hips and curves were accentuated, and small breasts were made to look more alluring; these women graced the windows. The men depended on fitted suits; their chests looked proud this way, and the linen fabric kept them from soaking wools to the point where they would faint from the heat.

The black women, wearing thin cotton dresses, laden with groceries in baskets, walked alongside their white mistresses. Others idled in doorways, avoiding doing the household chores if they possibly could.

Margarita walked along this street. She was almost thirty, a dark beauty; her expressive, black eyes were hidden amid silken, brown hair that she refused to pile atop her head unless she could not stand the heat. She moved toward a house with a green door where she hesitated, then knocked.

Mercedes, so voluptuous she spilled out of her starched servant's dress in several places, opened the door. The moment she saw Margarita, she worried. *What is a porcelain doll doing here?* she thought. Her brows knitted tightly and her back wrenched together. She was most likely younger than the young woman who stood before her, but she had the years of an old sage tucked inside her brain, and she used the thoughts as tools when she needed them. "Are you here to see Mr. Johnson?" Mercedes glanced at Isabel, who held her mother's hand in a tight grip.

Margarita nodded and smiled slightly. "Yes. I'm here for the job. The housekeeping job."

Mercedes hesitated, and Margarita began to panic. "I need this…a good job like this," she said in a low whisper.

"Come back this afternoon," Mercedes said. "I will talk to him before that."

Just after sunset, hours later, Mercedes allowed Margarita through the door and led her past the formal foyer: white plastered walls, the darkest tile for the floor. They moved deeper into the house, where pots of flowers lined the tiles, softening the place. But the rooms grew darker; the plantation shutters had turned the house cool as a cocoon.

Margarita, too, was there by accident. She had arrived in Cartagena from Santa Fe de Bogota nearly two months prior. The plans had been to stay for a few days while she, her husband, and their daughter, Isabel, now eight, waited for their boat to Barcelona.

The day of departure, Margarita and Isabel waited out the heat inside a small café. Isabel sipped an icy guava juice while her father went to the docks to see about tickets and boarding. When the hours passed and he had not returned, Margarita lifted Isabel into her arms and walked down the rambling street that led to the harbor. She found the dock man, his feet propped against the wall of the shipping office. He told her a man had dropped to his knees and was packed away just before sunset. Margarita could not comprehend what the man was saying and asked again and again, "Sent where?" her voice breaking more each time.

The man shrugged and stood to accept a small shipping container that was arriving. "He was dead," he said flatly. "I would not know."

Margarita was at the hospital thirty minutes later, hoping that everything was a mistake, but when her husband's body was showed to her, she faded away. It was not until Isabel start patting on her face that she awakened.

She sat with Isabel against the open wall of the hospital until dawn, when a thick mortician with braided hair told them she would call the police if they did not move.

Margarita spent every single penny she had left on her husband's funeral, and after walking every single street in the city, she found a job with a seamstress along the Calle Santo Domingo a day later. She was an expert with a needle, and the beadwork she did the first day convinced the seamstress that the women she clothed would be pleased. The business grew in healthy leaps within a month. But the promise the seamstress had made to her—to pay her more if this happened—was a lie.

Margarita was sixteen pesos short for rent that week. She wandered the long way home, sure she would find the answers before she arrived, but nothing came to her. She paused, holding her hands together so she wouldn't shake, and saw a woman posting on the far wall a small sign that read:

FOREIGN GENTLEMAN REQUIRES THE
SERVICES OF A HOUSEKEEPER.
FAIR WAGES. ROOM AND BOARD INCLUDED.

Margarita was led into the drawing room, where Indian statues and oak furniture upholstered in leather were carefully arranged. Mercedes left her far too quickly; she glanced back, thinking maybe she would follow, but kept her feet glued to the tile floor.

Meanwhile, Samuel Johnson was watching Margarita from a room that lay against the far corner and to the side. He glanced at her once, then took a step back and eyed her more thoroughly in safe shadows. He admired her soft skin, the way her dress hugged her lean frame, her neck, her chin, and the way her hair cascaded along her shoulders like waves. A breath of satisfaction filled him.

Then, as if perfectly timed and choreographed, he entered the room. She did not see him until he was just past her shoulder. Like a bird, she was temporarily stunned.

"Buenos días," he said simply.

"Buenos días, Señor Johnson."

He studied her again. She had a delicate pair of hands—not a cook's hands at all. Nor were they those of a worker, but maybe of an artisan, a trade he thought useless.

Her eyes darted up. "I don't mind the kind of job this is, so you understand. I need to make a living. I have a six-year-old daughter."

"I see. No husband?"

At first she did not look at him directly, but soon she looked up at him and shook her head. "I assure you, my daughter, she won't be—"

"When can you begin?" he asked, cutting her short.

⁓

Margarita washed dishes in the deep porcelain sink and watched Isabel stand precariously on a chair on the far wall, reaching for a glass inside a cabinet. Mercedes plucked a chicken while she sat along the tiled wall.

"Such a big house," Margarita said idly. "How you have worked this? All this yourself. It's heavy labor."

"I did not ask him for help."

"No?"

"No. You are going to fricassee the bird, you said?"

"No—Yes—Is this a mistake? How does he like it?"

"Fricassee is his favorite. There were several women who came, and Mr. Johnson turned them all down. Very capable cooks." Mercedes arrived at the sink. Margarita was certain Mercedes was going to let loose with insults, though that was not her aim at all. "He goes out after supper. He doesn't go to see friends. He drinks with the peasants, at Don Felipe's cantina." Her voice dropped into a harsh, gossipy whisper. "And then, they say, his tongue goes black."

Margarita was thoroughly frightened. Her back went stiff. Mercedes smiled like a cat, knowing what effect she had just had on Margarita. She stood upright and called out to Isabel, "Be careful with that!" Margarita looked around and saw Isabel standing stock-still with a small jar in her hands, which Mercedes abruptly snatched from her. Margarita saw a skull-and-crossbones symbol clearly labeled on the bottle.

Isabel looked to her mother, who admonished her silently.

"Mr. Johnson, he goes out after supper," Mercedes said to Margarita. "He doesn't see friends; at least, I don't think he does. And he takes that black box with him."

"What black box?" Margarita asked.

"The one he has in the living room."

"Ahh—the photo camera, you mean?"

"Yes." Mercedes's voice turned to a hiss. "I don't care what they say. There's witchcraft in that box."

Margarita hid her smile and continued to wash. Several moments passed before she found the courage to talk again. "What terrible things does Mr. Johnson say?"

"About his wife. How she died." She left the last bit for the longest time. "He killed her, he says. The witches who keep him company, they think it's just him pretending he's the devil himself—an efrit. That he believes it makes him alluring…" She stared at Margarita. "But I am here, every day, of every week." She paused before beginning the laundry. "I believe every word. Every one."

PART TWO

THE WAY
THE WIND
BLOWS

CHAPTER TEN

Sea Girt, New Jersey, 1890

Joseph's need for books began when he was fourteen, when he lost his baby fat and his childhood innocence, when loneliness hit his heart and he needed a way out. He craved stories more than most forlorn children. He had learned how steadfast stories could be. He was a friendless boy, thin-boned, pale, and sound-less—more a listener than a talker. He felt completely abandoned most days. He could walk the halls of his school and never inspire anyone's notice. To exchange a word with another student was rare.

He retreated from the world on the afternoons he was allowed and as soon as he was excused from the supper table at night. His nanny gave him all the books he wanted, so three active piles were beside his bed at all times. One was made up of adventure stories—Walter Scott, Robert Louis Stevenson, and Alexandre Dumas were favorites of his. In fact, he had read *The Count of Monte Cristo* so many times he could recite every phrase on demand. He also had a pile devoted just to science fiction. After reading Jules Verne, he would lie under the sheets, his bedside candle still aflame, and draw diagrams of the fantastical inventions the books conjured up.

He immersed himself in history books as well, and he had an odd affinity for texts, the kind found on the shelves at The Royal Astronomical Society or at Eton or Cambridge. When he first read them in the reading rooms at the British Library, or when the bookseller arrived with new editions, he pored over science experiments, his small fingers tracing the words again and again until he understood their meanings. He would then race home and attempt, with the help of kitchen staff, to do the simplest ones: experiments that illuminated gravity's pull, medical tests that would confirm a migraine headache. He read these odd books with such relish that his nurse and the house staff were certain he would ask to become a chemist, or possibly a doctor. Thus, when he was a bit older, his nurse went into her carriage and ordered the books he had asked for from a distinctive science bookseller in South London.

Books were Joseph's way of finding new worlds to conquer. For he was sure, as an unpopular boy abandoned by his own father—which was public knowledge—that he was considered… unnecessary. He had little doubt he would have much of a chance conquering this world at all.

That attitude changed as he grew and his physical strength fueled his confidence. He spurted to above six feet, two inches, in his fourteenth year alone. His shoulders stretched once he began playing rugby, and he could easily stand up to the severe boys at school. But he never, ever stopped with books. They were his best friends by then: utterly dependable, honest, forthright, and true. More than that, what he learned in them were invaluable weapons. Intelligence grew within him, and he built a body of knowledge that protected him from slurs. He could tell the ignorant from the authentic in a sentence.

Joseph took the mare out at dawn. The horse's icy exhales mixed with his, even as sweat gleamed on the lively mare's coat. They took the gravel roads this time so he would get to town faster. He knew it was too early to call on anyone properly, but he hoped Dr. Edwards, being used to strange hours, would accept this and allow him in.

Dr. Edwards answered the front door himself. He was the second one up; only Millicent was awake, churning butter and singing softly into her morning tea.

"Good morning, Joseph," he said as he watched the lad tie the mare to the front garden gate. "It's barely—"

"Six o'clock. I know. Is it all right that I come in?"

"Yes, of course." Out of habit, Dr. Edwards looked for signs of abnormality and saw nothing but a young man, cold, impatient, red-eared, tearing his riding gloves off too fast. "Are you not well?" he asked, to be certain.

"No physical complaints, I promise." Joseph smiled. But it was a troubled smile. He had something he needed to talk about; that was clear.

Dr. Edwards ushered the young man in and closed the door, sealing out the morning chill. He helped Joseph out of his coat and led him into his office. "I heard first music has been chosen for the wedding?"

"Yes—no—I'm not sure, to be honest. My father does not involve me in these decisions. I asked, but he refused me…I came to talk about Isabel."

"What is it?"

Joseph paused for a moment. He sensed Dr. Edwards' voice turn thin—tight, even. *Why would he be impatient so quickly on the subject?* he thought.

"She seems so…well."

"Yes? That is good to hear."

"Not the slightest symptom of tuberculosis. What stage did you say she is entering?"

"I need to check my notes. I see several patients every day. I'm sure you know that."

"Yes, of course."

"But if I did, I cannot share that information with you. It's the oath I take. What happens between a doctor and his patient is wholly private and confidential."

"Would you look at her again, please?"

"Can you explain to me what has you so agitated, Joseph?"

Joseph stood and paced before Dr. Edwards. "There is something—off. I know it. She acts so defensive, but she is also frightened. She won't admit this. She hides behind this angry mask, but it's clear she feels hunted."

Joseph expected an immediate answer from the doctor, and when he didn't get one, he stopped and looked closely at the man. The silence between them now was truly uncomfortable. Dr. Edwards was not sure whether to offer Joseph tea or not. "I have seen many cases of tuberculosis."

"Yes, I'm sure. But something is amiss here. I can feel it." He patted his heart. "There should be a chronic cough; there is none. I was with her for at least three hours the other day—"

Edwards cut him off quickly. "You were with her?"

Joseph nodded.

"That was unwise, Joseph."

"She displays no fever. She has the healthiest glow. She has kept her weight, and her eyes are not the least bit rheumy. She is isolated there in that cabin. She is lonely."

"Joseph. Stop."

"I don't believe she is even ill…I don't."

"There were high fevers, Joseph. She coughed up blood."

"There could be any number of causes for that—bronchial fever, pneumonia—which is highly similar. There are tropical viral fevers that have a high rate of survival. Maybe she has a hereditary condition—"

"Is this your diagnosis that you are giving me?" Dr. Edwards asked pointedly.

Joseph realized how aggressive his language had become. He did not want Dr. Edwards to think he did not respect his experience, but he had slipped past the bounds of appropriate behavior the day before when spending the entire morning with Isabel. He had made her laugh several times with his stories of his London boy brawls; he left out the stories where he had not won, and of the ingenious ways he found to end the fight before his nose was cracked or a rib was split. He had asked her as many questions as she would allow. He could see clearly one thing: she felt caged. His father had allowed her to have some education, but it was limited to the fundamentals. Aside from Elizabeth and Sarah, who was more a governess than a friend, she lived wholly inside her head.

She was so lively, though, so thoroughly quick, but not in a clever way. She was real, filled with need; just no purpose. Her voice, a soft, husky alto, made him drunk. He began to pick up on how she moved, the way she cocked her head to the side as she listened to him talk, the way she ignored herself, unaware of her effect on men, on him, on how his heart beat so hard when able to get within a few feet of her that his ribs ached. He knew this key fact about her: she was not drawn to outward human shapes. Faces, hips, legs—these did not interest her at all. She looked beyond that, straight into the heart.

No one as sick as Dr. Edwards said she was could focus beyond their own pain. Joseph convinced himself of that as he tossed in his bed that night. "Will you see her again, Dr. Edwards?" he had asked him. "I can come with you."

"I've just told you, what happens between a doctor and patient is private, Joseph. You must respect that."

Joseph nodded, but his eyes burned. "I have two names from Philadelphia. I can arrange for them to come."

Dr. Edwards got up instantly. "Then why do you need me?"

"Someone should have taken her to be properly diagnosed."

"She *was!*" Dr. Edwards stopped himself. "I suggest you badger your own father with your medical inquiry. Now, if you'll excuse me, my first patient will arrive at any moment, and I have to prepare."

Sarah watched Samuel Johnson finish dressing for the day. She never wanted to know more than she needed to about his past. She had heard stories—some wild, some not—about his time in London. She had been told that he and his wife had agreed long ago that she would remain in England with the son and he would live in America, but she also thought that could be fiction. She knew he had gone to see them more than once. Maybe they had argued? Couples did that. About what, she never could divine on her own. The wife disappeared, it was said, after Mr. Johnson's last journey there. He left Joseph there in the care of the house staff. But this, too, was all gossip. Samuel never offered any information, and no one dared ask. Nothing ever appeared in the papers; no one knew first-hand what had occurred.

The man she worked for was shrouded in hats that made him appear as if he had just slits for eyes. He was wary; stony on the worst of days. He never spoke of anything intimate, so Sarah had no idea who the man was, other than his daily schedule and the commands he leveled at her. His cool, voracious demeanor sometimes ruffled her. When Isabel began to come of age, she began to slip out of her shadow, and Sarah saw the parts of Mr. Johnson that were white with heat. Isabel could twist his temper with one look, and, as she became a teen, she spoke to the man of the house as if he were a raider, not her guardian. Sarah fought back tears on the nights when he would snap and take a belt to Isabel's hide. She cried out, but Mr. Johnson never wavered. He let the leather dig scars into her backside, leaving wounds so deep they never fully healed.

This never stopped the girl, despite Sarah's best efforts to silence her. Isabel's singed, clipped answers, on days she could see that Mr. Johnson was already strained, were pure genius, mixed with utter stupidity. Isabel could turn the temperature inside the man to scorching. After he had beaten her, he could be heard throwing things. Sarah would stand ramrod-straight, hear it happen, then run recklessly to see, only to find the room empty and the shattered china against the wall or the glass in the leaded windows cracked like a spider's web.

Sarah entered his room as Mr. Johnson stroked the scar before turning to see her. "Is there anything that goes on in this house that you don't know about, Sarah?"

"I doubt it, sir."

"The smallest cockroach is at your mercy."

"Hope so, sir. I like to run a tight ship."

"So no secrets, yes?"

She looked up. He was standing in the door; he used his arms to hold the frame while he leaned in toward her. She felt like taking a step backwards but didn't think it wise to show her fear. "No, sir. Not if I can help it."

He looked at her hard for a moment and then turned his back. "You tell me everything, and I will be sure. You leave out anything, any small fact, thinking you can make that decision for me, and it will be a mistake." He did not turn around to see if he had scared her. He knew he had, which calmed him, for that was his aim. "I'm here all day, doing the books. I don't want to be disturbed."

"Yes, of course." She had trouble getting the words out. But it did not matter. He had passed her and was halfway down the stairs by that point.

⁂

Joseph lifted the bottle of champagne from the cold waves. He had slipped it into his coat and spent the next hour walking the shore-line as the bottle chilled. When he sensed the effervescent bubbles had risen, he slipped the bottle into the leather pouch behind the saddle, placed the two glasses he had stolen into his waistband, and set off atop the mare.

He had spent the day walking the orchards—thinking, mostly. He had stopped a few times to help workers carry heavy bushels into their wagons. One worker had been slow with a sore ankle, and Joseph had wrapped it tightly so that the man could hobble to his mule without wincing. But the rest of the day had been spent alone. He had left the Edwards' house earlier without waiting for Elizabeth to wake, leaving just his card. He should have; he knew that. He knew it would create problems, but he pushed them aside. He wrestled instead with the hundreds of erratic feelings that came and went. Sometimes it felt as if they invaded his head all at once: images of her, that soft lemon scent, the low timbre of her anger. His doubts—whether he was wrong about her illness, if she would ever consider, even for one moment, being near him—also created chaos. His head would easily explode if he let the doubts linger.

He was anxious to see the specialists in Philadelphia, but would she even agree to go? When he had left her the day before, he could sense in her movements that she had begun to slowly gravi-tate toward him. Like an orphaned animal, she used her senses to direct her thoughts. She watched his eyes, the way he moved. She had begun to ask questions about what his childhood was like. She never asked why he was here—he was sure she knew, but it was the last thing he wanted to discuss. No. Elizabeth was off limits for him, at least for the moment. He needed time to find his way in, then once that happened…

What if these thoughts he had were delusional? Was he going mad and didn't know it? That thought made him laugh.

"If this is insanity," he said aloud, "then I welcome it. Please. I want more."

∽∽

He saw her walking along the dunes, her hair behind her like a sail, her hips swaying gently as she worked her way up the slope to reach the cabin. She gripped what looked like wild herbs in one hand, and her wide-brimmed straw hat was tied around her waist. He was leaning against the pillar of the cabin, his arms folded across his chest, his ankles crossed casually.

"Are we friends, yet?" he called out to her when she saw him. "Or are you going to try to shoot me again?"

She stopped, covering her eyes with her hand to see him properly, and then walked up to the porch without giving him an answer.

∽∽

"Up at the house, everybody thinks about music, and cakes, and wedding guests…" He pulled the champagne glasses from behind him and shifted his weight so she could see the open champagne bottle tucked into the sand. "They've completely forgotten it's my birthday."

She stopped and watched how his eyes softened; they turned down at the outer edges, so she could not help but move closer. Was he hurt? She wasn't sure—he might be trying to fool her. Most men, she found, tried to mislead her in some way. The boys who

77

worked in the orchard, several of them, one after the other, had attempted to lure her into the trees, trap her and pull her down into the dirt so they might scrape their sore, calloused hands over her. They came up with the stupidest lies. So did the older men, the ironworks foremen, though they were cleverer with their tactics. But it was easy to read the greedy lust on their faces. Nothing they told her had the least effect. She had turned it all down, kicking them between the legs—hard, if need be—to make her point.

Here, she wasn't sure anymore. He seemed…exposed, as if he willed her to take the rifle and use it. His expression was a mix of tortured pain, utter anguish…and sheer joy. Even before he spoke, she saw how his eyes were glued to her when she approached. And there was a regard for what she told him, as if the words she spoke were to be believed. But he also might be off his feet. He was using the pillar as a leaning post.

"How much have you been drinking?" she asked him.

"Not enough," he replied, then: "A bit…I'm fine. I wanted to wait for you. What is the point of having a birthday drink by myself? It's just that you make me nervous, so I steadied my nerves before I came."

"Where is Elizabeth? She would like to celebrate with you, I am sure."

He dropped his head. "Yes. Very practical thought." Elizabeth was the one thing she shouldn't, couldn't bring up—because he had no answers. He worked on it obsessively, but he still had not found the answers.

He came closer, but he already felt defeated. He was sure she would pass him by and go inside the cabin alone. Instead, she slipped her hand behind him, lifted the second glass from the sand, and held out the empty glass to him, waiting. He smiled, bent down for the bottle, and filled her glass. "Careful," he said, leaning in to whisper this. "You want to keep your wits about you. I don't fully trust myself—being here." She smiled at him, not frightened away this time, but amused.

He filled his own glass and then let the rims touch quietly. "I have found something we have in common, then."

"Yes? What?"

"A love for the impractical."

She made them a light supper, which they had eaten as they sat on the log near the dunes. They had roasted small lobsters, warm bread Sarah had brought, and berries from the orchard, drizzled in honey. Joseph watched as she returned from the cabin with a book in her hand. She offered it to him when she sat down.

"Is this—?" He opened the cover and let his fingers drift over the pages.

"Yes. I stole it from the Johnson house library many years ago, and when I was sent down here, I made Sarah bring all my books down to me."

"You weren't lying. There are all five first editions."

The book was *The Three Musketeers*. The linen pages looked as if they had come from a monastery, hand-drawn. They were thick and inked in the most illustrious style.

"This should be encased in glass inside the Victoria and Albert in London, or in the Vatican vaults," he said.

"No." She took the book from him and looked at the magnificent pages. "Books are meant to be…" She searched for the right word.

"Family," he said simply.

She looked up at him. It was the perfect choice of word. "Yes," she said happily. "Mysterious friends, too. Sarah would read to me when I was young, so I would learn English. She would sit at the side of my bed and say, 'What does this word mean?' She knew that when she found books from the library missing, she would eventually find them stuffed in a pillowcase in my closet."

"A good coconspirator, Sarah."

"She never said a word. She just waited for the books to return to their place on the shelf." She paused for a moment. "I would not have known anything had it not been for her—and Elizabeth, of course. But this one I never returned."

He took two of his fingers and let them rest on her chin, and then slowly he lifted it so her eyes met his. "Isabel. Your eyes…" He had to swallow before he had the courage to say the next words. "They stop my heart."

Isabel twisted so she could free herself, but this time Joseph refused to let her go. He guided her by the cheek to look at him once more. "Let me…" He grazed his thumb against her bottom lip. "Please say you will let me…at least just look?"

She fought back a tear. As it escaped down her cheek, he brushed it away. "Don't cry. Please. I won't if you don't want me to. I promise. You aren't sick, though. I know it. I am sure of it. You can't be."

She felt her eyes glisten, and that was all he needed. She took his shoulders and pulled him in, letting his mouth envelop hers.

Dr. Edwards paced the Johnson foyer, wearing out the rug before Sarah returned to show him into the study. He found Samuel Johnson's desk covered in documents. Ledgers were open, with a pen devoted to each book. Samuel had his back to the door when Edwards entered. Johnson was studying a diagram. It looked like a schematic drawing of the ironworks factory, but Edwards could not be sure.

"Edwards, I have little time today. Sit. Tell me what you need."

"Isabel."

"What about her?"

"Joseph came to see me about her." Johnson turned then. "He has many questions. Most of which center around the fact that she does not appear ill at all. He is—"

Edwards hesitated.

"Speak," Johnson demanded.

"Wildly inquisitive," was all Edwards could come up with.

Johnson paused and, without even the slightest hint of emotion, said, "You rejected my plan. Now she remains. Whose fault is that?"

Edwards chilled at the memory of that conversation; he did not ever take Samuel Johnson for granted. He knew what Samuel was capable of: the thoughts, the off-hand comments over the years, about women, about their purpose. Johnson had ice in his veins. So Edwards tried to push past that night when Johnson's idle suggestion that Isabel be "removed" had been raised. Edwards's protestations were so swift, yet he remembered none of then. He could barely stand the memory without strong bouts of nausea.

"Your son has some of your traits. He doesn't like being told things; that is one, Samuel. He told me straight out that Isabel has been misdiagnosed. I regret doing anything at all about this, Samuel. I am a reputable physician."

"Who is questioning your reputation? No one in this house."

"I just told you, Samuel. Your son. And if he gives up…someone else will also ask. It was a stupid plan, and I regret offering it. It's obvious she is not ill…and while I have agreed to do things for you in the past—"

"*Christ*!" Edwards jumped at the roar in Samuel's voice. "Stop whining! It's inconsequential! She's just the daughter of a fucking whore! If it becomes obvious, I will deal with it, all right?"

"I did this to *save her,* Samuel. Otherwise, I was convinced you would—"

They both froze.

"I would do what, Edwards?" Samuel smiled.

Edwards refused to finish his thought.

Samuel poured them each a brandy. "Women. Their roots rest in hell—you know it. I know it. These stories Joseph brings to you, they come from her. She has poisoned his thoughts, clearly." He looked at the doctor once again and then went back to his schematics, where he felt much more at home. "I said I will handle it."

Joseph sat on the edge of his bed, his body bent in thought. He thought the lightning outside, an early spring storm that had brushed across the shoreline an hour earlier, surrounded the house with cymbals. The last thunderclap was loud enough to split the roof; it felt as though it cracked open his skull as well. When Joseph heard the piercing clap a second time, this one felt like a hot poker. He forced himself upright and twisted around to see it was no clap at all but his father, whose open palm was red and sore.

"What are you doing?" Joseph was incredulous.

"Explain what *you* think *you* are doing!" Samuel spat back.

"About?" Joseph sounded strangely calm.

Without warning, Samuel slammed his open palm against Joseph's head. "Do *not* toy with me!" He loomed over Joseph now, rolling one sleeve up, then thinning the sweat from his brow. "You accuse a man—a venerable doctor for three decades—of subverting his profession, of being no more than a—a shyster? A man who will, in a short time, be family? It defies logic. Tell me. What do you know about medicine? As I recall, you study law."

"She is not sick."

"You have *no* idea what you are doing, do you?"

Joseph stood up now, eye to eye with his father. "No. And yes."

Samuel slammed his son's body against the far wall. When Joseph groaned and roared as he pushed forward, Samuel hit him as hard as he could across the eyes, blinding him. Joseph bent forward, sheltering his face in his hands.

"I will say this now, and then it will not be revisited again. Understood? You will not see Isabel again. You will not visit that house."

"Why?."

"You will *not* speak to anyone else about her."

"Why does she threaten you?"

"Threaten me? Threaten *me*?" He left Joseph crouched against the wall. "You are confused! *I* am the one who threatens!" he thundered as he stretched both his fists to the ceiling, leaving the bedroom door wide open as he rocked down the hall. "*I am the one who threatens! Yes?*" he shouted to the walls as he passed, filled with an uproarious burst of electricity that lit him from within, this pure, undiluted rage. He could have erupted into flames right then and it would not have been a surprise.

CHAPTER ELEVEN

Elizabeth made a perfect cup of tea. She knew just how long to steep the leaves in the teapot, and just how much milk and sugar to add for those with a sweet tooth. She was taught well. These were the things her mother did for her and they could easily talk about with each other; whatever interested Elizabeth beyond entertaining would turn her mother to stone and cause her to resent Elizabeth for even bringing it up.

That was what Isabel was for—all other things; hence a way to understand the larger world. Elizabeth rarely doubted what was told her at home; she mostly took household belief as fact. Sometimes when Elizabeth offered an idea, it ended in fights at the supper table, with one parent or the other mimicking Elizabeth, dubious that she was intelligent enough to come up with even one original thought. She always went silent after that. Why Isabel made Elizabeth feel safe was an interesting puzzle, then. Isabel questioned everything and was a risk to be around. But Elizabeth was sure that if the world ended tomorrow, Isabel would be the first person she would run to.

Elizabeth was captivated by the lyrical sounds the strange Spanish language offered. Conversely, Isabel loved the exact qualities English words proffered, for English speakers never talked as if they were whispering a poem or a prayer.

When Elizabeth asked Isabel to teach her a language, she knew it was something that could easily get them both into serious trouble. But she knew how free it made Isabel feel, how it offered her the chance to be something she could never be in North America. Elizabeth loved being able to give her that. Isabel teased Elizabeth about her wooden accent, but little by little she began to link the words into meaning and they would talk to each other on long walks along the beach, on horseback, and during hide-and-seek games inside the Johnson orchard.

They had never agreed to keep this a secret—Isabel never asked her to, and she never offered. She was sure she didn't need to. Isabel trusted her to never betray her. Elizabeth bought them both books to read; she would learn more words this way, and Isabel would be allowed underhanded pleasures. No one ever asked her, not once over the course of many years, why and how Elizabeth knew how to read Spanish novels; they had all assumed she only looked at the pictures.

She was reading one such book when Joseph arrived. "En aquella tarde de primavera…" she said softly to herself. "El mar lucia mas profundo que nunca." She had not picked up a book in ages, but today she felt in the mood to do so.

She poured Joseph his tea. He smiled gratefully and waited for it to cool. He had said little upon arrival, and nothing about what had infested her thoughts, namely the early morning visit with her father the day before. She barely knew the man, and took the silence between them to study him: he was uncommonly handsome, broad across the shoulders, the deepest green eyes, large hands he used softly. He was also funny, well-read, and easy to believe. He was chosen for her and she had said yes before she ever laid eyes on him. He seemed kind, but he never once looked at her, right at her—the way she imagined someone should if he truly felt…if the two of them truly were….

"Is your tea all right?" He had not touched it yet, and she was worried.

"Yes, perfect, thank you." He looked up at her, and she stiffened suddenly. The way he looked; she could swear he had pity in his eyes. "Elizabeth—" he began, and halted again.

She smiled broadly. "I am not as inquisitive as you, as you know, but I have had a taste for puzzles."

His eyes lit, then narrowed. "How do you know that about me? I have never said anything, have I? Did my father tell you that?"

"Maybe. I'm not sure. I might have just guessed."

"It was a very good one." He said this so easily.

"I wanted to know the roots of what brought us together." She felt as if she were talking aloud to herself now, not actually to another person. "A puzzle, of sorts. What brought our parents to this decision? I know it's not necessary for a young woman to know these things. She must rely that her parents have chosen the match with caution and intelligence." She paused. "But I do wonder, regardless."

"And what do you come up with?"

She looked at him for a long time before she spoke. "There is a letter. A letter from Colombia addressed to Mr. Johnson. My father has it in his office…I don't know what it says exactly, but I believe he's been blackmailing Mr. Johnson for years. My father must feel he needs to keep it. I don't know how he got hold of it…it must have been very difficult, considering."

Elizabeth let her guard fall for a moment. "I'd have liked to meet you in other circumstances, Joseph. But I feel that if we get married…it may be that one day, we'd feel like we were part…of a crime."

A few moments later, she was inside her father's office. She looked at the big wooden box in one of the corners. It was closed and secured with a big lock, impossible to open, she thought in that moment. She sifted through the folders in the desk, listed alphabetically: The *G*'s, *H*'s, *I*'s…then to the *J*'s. She turned and looked at Joseph, who was leaning against the office doorframe. He looked at her with true wonder and respect. She felt shy suddenly; her cheeks bloomed, and she hid a mischievous smile as she pulled one more folder out of its place and gave him a nod.

Joseph had barely moved from his place in his father's study. He needed air to breathe, and he felt as if he could get none. Being in this room made him feel as if he might suffocate. The letter Elizabeth had told him about earlier was seared into his brain. He had left her with barely a goodbye and hung atop his mare as they walked slowly back to the Johnson house. It took him more than an hour and a half, and even after he had arrived, he had waited at the front gate, certain he did not want to go any further.

He had been slumped in the chair for an hour or more. He had rifled through drawers, scanned papers, absorbed as much as quickly as he could. He ran on a hot cord of enraged energy, though his body felt weak and his head ached. He halted all of the searching and ransacking upon noticing a small box sitting on a top shelf.

"Hullo, Joseph," he heard his father say. It was menacing, that monotone…a tense calm that pulled at the hairs on the back of Joseph's neck.

"I didn't know you were home," Joseph said without looking up. "Do you know where my passport is? I was looking for it earlier and can't find it."

Samuel stood silently, not answering his son. Joseph picked up the box and offered it to his father. "I remember this at home, in London. It was my mother's, yes?"

Samuel stared at the box. "Yes." He opened it and gazed at a small tiara covered in diamonds. "She wore it the day we married. Would you like to give it to Elizabeth?"

Joseph only watched as the diamonds danced along the walls of the library.

Cartagena, Colombia, 1880

Mercedes opened the door to find the police commissioner. She knew him not by name, but from the gossiping women in the market. He loomed over her like a bear and was heavyset from head to toe; clearly, he liked his food and wine. The commissioner had been to the house once before; it had been late at night, and Mercedes had to dress quickly. She had waited a few moments before finding the courage to open the door herself. That time, the commissioner had dispensed with any greeting, walking inside toward the back of the house, where Johnson was. She had remained awake until just before dawn, her nose flaring at the strong smell of rum and smoke wafting down the hall. She had peered out to see the commissioner leaning this way and that while opening and closing the front door.

"I'll let Mr. Johnson know you're here," she said without meeting his eyes. She led him into the cool sitting room and left him there. When Johnson appeared a few minutes later, the commissioner had sunk deep into the cushions of a wide chair.

"Good afternoon, Commissioner," Johnson said evenly.

"How are you, Mr. Johnson? I am guilty. I have been remiss in not coming to call for a long time."

Johnson waved his hand aimlessly. "Colombia works on its own clock."

"Good thought. True thought. How goes the writing of your book? How does the sea air treat you? Good for the heart and the lungs, no?"

"All of the above."

Margarita brought them a tray of lemonade and laid out a small stack of powdered sugar cookies on linen napkins. The eyes of both men followed her closely before they looked at each other again. Then their smiles widened.

"I have an uncommonly handsome household, do I not?" All the commissioner could do was let out a hearty laugh.

They walked together after a long, leisurely supper. In Cartagena, the commissioner lived off the spoils of the wealthy— excellent rums and beers; wine cellars had been particularly good the past few years. They all entertained him, fed him, bribed him generously. Johnson's kitchen staff was exceptionally talented; he wondered a few times if it was the soft, pudding-like woman who cooked or the other one, the frightened one, who refused to look him or Mr. Johnson in the eye. Her kittenish qualities and her timid, shaky way of walking made him want to rub his oily hands on her to see how she writhed. He didn't mind an anxious woman; it never put him off or stopped him from taking what he wanted. In fact, fear in a woman was an attractive quality; it made things more…memorable. The commissioner liked a memorable fuck when he could get one.

He was fairly sure he and Mr. Johnson had this trait in com-mon—this magnetic, slightly irrational pull they both felt toward innocent creatures. He could see it in Johnson's face, even as he watched him look at women as they passed, when the lit candles on the Johnson veranda cast spidery shadows on his vicious eyes. Johnson liked a hunt; anything less probably bored him.

The walk they enjoyed took them along the harbor, where the fishing boats were docked and the mongers' barrels were turned on their heads. The brine that preserved caught fish pooled around both the men's thick shoes.

They stopped for a bit to listen to the sounds of drums. The Africans who had made their way through the slave trade in one piece were on the beach. A group had formed around several men who used their hands and their feet to beat, twist, and writhe to the cannibalistic beats, their instruments dug into the damp sand.

"I admire a city with no codes," Johnson said after a while.

"And lucky for me, right? The fewer the codes, the more I'm needed. Mystery is my business. Cartagena keeps me rich and busy, both. The women especially. My tastes run to the exotic; this place suits me in that way."

They watched as a woman began to dance in front of the fire. She seemed bold, moving with the native rhythms of the fire, exhibiting carnal energy that egged the drummers to beat harder. But then the woman turned and her eyes met Johnson's. She could see the sheen of sweat that lined his brow. His eyes were the color of white spirits. She was frightened so badly she turned away and sat down on the sand a moment later, letting the tight rhythms roll away without her.

New York City, 1890

New York teemed only one time each day: before nightfall. No one met the others' eyes. Their heads were bowed, three-deep along the sidewalks; they wanted nothing more than to rush through the rain, find their street, escape the soot that settled along the curbs where the carriages idled, and slip inside their homes.

Johnson moved among them silently. He had a certain pattern he deemed necessary on these trips: he would take a horse into town, leave the animal in the care of a stable he trusted near the harbor, and wind his way uptown via two, three, sometimes four carriages. He wanted little evidence of his pathway and wanted less to meet anyone he knew.

He used the same brothel each time: a moody place along the Hudson, abandoned-looking, which suited the owner just fine. Anything that went wrong inside at night—and that happened all too often—was easy to fix. A limp, wrecked body could be dumped. Broken women could be sent away, even via the front door, for the house had few neighbors save for a fishmonger to the south and a carpenter's studio to the north.

The brothel was owned by a whore from Zacatecas whom Johnson had met during his travels. The woman welcomed the extra money Johnson pressed into her hands when he had gone too far, when doctors had to be called to nurse the disgusting wounds he had caused. The owner never questioned his tastes, as she called them; never said a word. To prove her loyalty she had local tequilas, the ones he favored, shipped from Mexico and Costa Rica, just for his pleasure. She would let him sit and drink on her shabby couch when he needed to calm his heart after his bad behavior left him unbalanced and in need of a numbing.

The woman with whom Johnson walked the stairs had chosen this room, for it meant she did not have to see what occurred; it did not yet have electricity. She chose this room when it suited, when a customer paid upfront and wanted several hours of…play. She found him interesting—alluring, even—but also made sure a room like this was far from the others. Men who looked foul, the way he certainly did, were to be handled with care.

She had offered at first to let him lead; it made her feel more secure. But he insisted he follow, so she was forced to feel his presence without being able to see what he was doing. She could feel hot breath on her neck. He did not look low-rent to her; his suit was bespoke, and his boots and gloves were of the finest leather.

She closed the door, undressed quickly, and waited silently on the edge of the bed for him to follow. He undressed and folded his clothes neatly on the bare dresser. She had only the candle to light the room, and when he turned in one movement to snuff the flame between his two reddened fingers, she inhaled sharply. He grabbed the back of her neck, taking a fistful of her hair in his grip, tugging her backwards. He slammed his wet lips over her mouth, then leaned into her, massaging himself harshly. He threw her back, and her head hit the headboard with a sharp *crack!*

He used his other hand to press her chest-bone down; the only reason why anyone would do this would be to crush the ribs. He did not caress her, nor did she even think he felt her touch. Instead, he pulled his upper hand free, stroked himself angrily again, let out a low, very slow growl, and punctured her against the mattress.

It took much longer than she had hoped. Twice, three times she rose from the mattress and he pulled her down, saying, "Not yet!" Over the course of two or more hours, she finally tried again and lifted herself up, resting her hands on her cheeks. She felt weak, drained. It was not that the man had exploited her, but that he was vengeful.

She let tears fall aimlessly off her cheeks while he dressed, placed the money on the mattress, and left without a word.

CHAPTER TWELVE

Sea Girt, New Jersey, 1890

Isabel did not wake instantly. It was nearly dawn, and the pounding on her door went on for long minutes before she was aware enough to understand what was happening. When she did, she lifted herself quickly to sitting. She listened at first, holding her arms around her knees. The pounding grew louder, then louder again, and then Joseph's voice, a mixture of torture and distress, made her sit up ramrod-straight.

"Isabel, please," he begged. "Open the door."

She rose, covering herself with a shawl. When she reached the door, she leaned against the wood, trying to discern what was wrong.

"I am aching to see you," she heard him say. The words went through the cracks like a whisper. His desperation made her smile slightly. She pushed away from the wall and opened the door for him.

He did not rush in; he stood stock-still, his eyes locked on her. At first he was angry that she had left him in the cold for as long as she had. She liked to see him suffer, he was sure of it. But he was so relieved when she arrived that any anger melted, leaving only the soft, dark circles under his eyes.

Finally, he spoke. "You have made me lovesick." It was a half-hearted accusation, and she reacted by cocking her hip slightly, one hand settled, showing him mock disgust. This was a teasing look, and he knew it, but he had no humor. "Don't mock me," he said. Her smile faded and she stood upright. She could see he was in true pain, and her smile disappeared altogether. "My ears ring," he said. "I hear nothing anyone says to me."

"Good. Now leave me alone." She looked at him but then looked down, wishing she had not said that.

He leaned in fast before she could move away, bracing himself against the doorframe. "Have the decency"—he lifted his hand to her cheek and forced her to look at him squarely—"to speak to my face." He was deadly serious, with not an ounce of mischief in his stance or his tone.

"I understand what you want," she said.

"Yes? What is that?"

"I am a woman."

"So I have noticed."

"You are like all the rest. I am sure of it." She stared at him now, wanting him to know little innocence was left inside her and he should not destroy what was left of it.

But what she saw in return surprised her. His eyes went black but he was hurt, deeply hurt. "Is that what you think of me? That I would be that way…with you?" He was clearly dumbfounded. He stayed where he was for a moment, but truly, his eyes told her he had retreated. He turned and left without a word.

She moved onto the porch, following him on instinct, but then stopped herself. *He looks wrecked,* she thought.

Joseph tried to stay as still as possible for the rest of the day. His head spun recklessly, and the dappled sunlight that danced across his room played cruel tricks on his imagination. He tried several times to prop his head up with his hands, but then thoughts of her invaded, and it was all he could do to stop from crying out for help.

He skipped supper, telling his father and Sarah the food would only make him more nauseous—which was true—and he lay in the dark, hoping for a small moment of peace.

He wasn't sure what shifted or why he went to the window. He opened his eyes, blinking once or twice, feeling the pain of a headache ringing his body. He lifted himself up on his elbows and watched the tree branches rake across the side of the house. This signified a new storm brewing. He watched it take the leaves up in bunches, letting them swirl above the roof. He rose and went to the window; stopped, and leaned in when the figure appeared beyond the trees along the edges of the south-facing orchard.

He watched for just one more moment, when the figure stopped, sensing the same thing he did—and she looked up. He felt his heart bang outside his chest. It was sudden, ferocious, this feeling. He did not wait it out; he raced right out the door.

His bare feet flew across the carpet, taking the stairs two, three, four at a time. He snatched his boots in the vestibule and flew out the door. He stopped, hopping on one foot while trying his best to shoe the other, while scanning the property for signs of her.

Once he spotted her, he was sure all it would take was one small shift, one slight change in a shadow to see her. And there it was: a light caught the heel of her foot as she slipped inside a row of peach trees. He took off fast, his booted feet barely touching the ground. He wanted her to see him, not be shocked into submission. He wanted her to know what was about to happen, to show him a sign that she would let him in.

He stopped along the row of trees. She had stopped as well, and when she turned, he could see her bare legs silhouetted against the moonlight. Her hair flew up into the air with a strong gust, and slowly, she opened to him. He smiled back, utterly grateful, and took off after her. When he reached her, he did not say a word. He just caught her hand, not gripping but pulling gently, gently… slowing her down until both of them stopped. She looked up at him. They were mere inches from each other. He had her face in his hands a second after that, and without asking, his lips crashed into hers. He wanted to find some sense of control. He let her go so he might try, but she held his bottom lip with her teeth, and he could not for the life of him catch his breath. Then, slowly, he let his tongue seduce her mouth open.

He wrapped both his hands under her thighs and lifted her up. "Wrap your legs around me," he commanded softly. She closed her eyes, let her head drop slightly in surrender, and did as he asked. He carried her this way back to the house, up the stairs, again two at a time, and into his room.

Isabel woke a few hours later. Her legs were tangled with Joseph's; she had been sleeping on his chest as he lay on his back. The slow thrumming of his heart was welcome, for she needed a small rest from the last few frantic hours when he had taken them both into a silent frenzy. Both had gasped for air several times, for he had to hold her close to him, insisting again and again, "Don't leave." He would say this at the slightest sense she was pulling away. He needed to feel what it was like to not just be inside her but to feel every muscle flex and spasm. They had gripped each other so hard they had become bruised—she on both hips, he across the shoulders and back. When she thought she had exhausted him he shook his head no, asking for more.

Lying in the dark, she felt weak, sated, and even a little dizzy. She looked about the room; it bordered on absurdity, being back inside this house again. The loneliness inside the cabin dogged her, but here she was in an iron cage, trapped, near suffocation. She sat up, wanting to leave suddenly, but she felt his hand drift up and wrap around her waist.

"Please don't."

"Don't what?" she asked, turning to look at him. His eyes were beseeching, wounded, even before she was able to move away.

"Don't leave the bed," he said simply. "Please."

She softened as if to agree, but when he loosened his grip, she moved away. He sat up instantly and leaned in. His kisses were not wanted at first, and she moved her face from right to left, avoiding him as best she could, but it never worked. He would not give up. He wanted her, and soon she admitted she wanted him, too. Her hands began to explore again, and when he let out a small moan of pleasure she twirled around, captured his legs in hers, straddled him, and leaned down to kiss him even deeper.

Cartagena, Colombia, 1880

Margarita rarely fell asleep before her daughter. Isabel had terrible nightmares. She was never sure what they were about or why they had come on, but they were fierce. Isabel would wake, her body soaked in sweat, and would shake for long minutes until Margarita assured her it was only a dream. She thought the first cure was to be sure Isabel's last thoughts before bed were peaceful. So they ended every day the same way: Margarita would hold her daughter close and sing as many songs as she asked for until the small girl's arms loosened their grip on her waist and her eyes grew heavy.

When they moved into Mr. Johnson's house, she had to leave Isabel to do her duties. She would often come back to her small room and find Isabel curled into a tight ball, not asleep, but not awake either. Though Margarita tugged at her, she refused to unravel. This house was clearly not a decent place for a child, and

Margarita would have to find a way to get them back home to Santa Fe de Bogota. She missed the icy air of the Andes and the family dinners that ended in quarrels. The money Mr. Johnson paid her was twice what she could get in any other house, but the fears it instilled in her and Isabel made her not care about the money any longer.

At the same time, she was grateful that Mercedes had become a friend—the three women felt like family—but she would begin her search for a new place as soon as she had a small amount of savings tucked away.

It was an hour after Isabel had finally drifted off to sleep. It was a hot night, the kind where the air lay deadly still and nothing moved. Their sheets were damp with Margarita's sweat. Isabel tossed a few times, banging her head against the wall that cornered the bed, which jolted her awake.

At that moment, she heard the steady creak of footsteps. She tensed, frightened and bewildered; no one came to this side of the house, especially not at night. Then, a moment later, the sounds stopped. She let out a breath and, just as suddenly, took a sharp breath in again.

Mr. Johnson filled the doorframe. She could smell brandy, piss, and mold. She sat up and cornered her body against the wall.

"I can't sleep," he said. "The heat."

She quickly circled her legs over the edge of the bed. Her thin wrap lay across a chair. It would take several steps to get to it. She froze, looking at it. "I will get you some mint tea," she said, her face glued to the floor. "It cools the body." She moved toward her wrap, but he anticipated this somehow and moved, half-pitching into her body.

"The darker the skin, the deeper the hole…" he said slowly. He took her by the shoulders, towered over her and, before she could utter a word, lifted her up and pinned her against the far wall. "The deeper the hole men fall into, I meant to say." His words were slurring, his breath stale and ugly. She ducked her head in defense, not wanting to look him in the face.

"Please," she whispered. "I don't want to."

He slammed into her and kneed himself in between her legs, pushing her open while lifting her higher up onto the wall. He leaned so hard on her she could barely breathe. His limp, wet lips pushed onto hers and pressed harder as his tongue pried her mouth open.

Margarita heard Isabel stir, and then moan.

"Mama?" Isabel asked softly.

"I am here." Margarita let loose a pained sob. She then pushed Mr. Johnson as hard as she could with her arms and forced herself to steady her voice. "Isabel…darling?" Isabel sat up in bed and gazed at the man, his shoulders leaning one way and then the other, and then at her mother. Margarita offered her arm to lure Isabel out of bed. "Go to see Mercedes, yes? She will let you sleep with her tonight."

Isabel did not move. She gripped the sheets with her fists. "I want to stay here."

"Isabel. Now, please. Señor Johnson and I must speak."

Isabel remained still. Then she shifted her legs off the bed and padded out the door.

Margarita waited for sounds indicating Isabel opening the door to Mercedes's room, and then she turned to face the man. He had begun to sweat profusely; his shirt was drenched, and sweat poured down both cheeks. She shivered, clutching herself, when she saw his eyes roll wholly back into his head before he moved toward her mouth. She gripped the dresser behind her and felt for the sewing scissors she kept in the top drawer.

He pushed his fingers along her cheekbones, poking them hard. "Your skin tastes like brine," he said as he licked up the jawbone. He pushed onto her again, his tongue in her mouth, his hard knees digging up into her torso. Her soft whimpers—of fear, pain—excited him further. He let go of her for a moment when she stuck her chest out, forcing him off-balance momentarily.

"It is true, then, what they are saying?" she asked in a hiss.

Not caring to answer, he forced his fingers and then his tongue inside her mouth. Then he felt the scissors pinch. He grabbed her face and drew back, feeling the hot stick of blood.

"They say you are the evil—that you killed your wife," she said as her tears rolled past her chin and landed on her breasts.

He smiled; proud of what she had called him. "I am…an unbeliever," he said flatly. He knew he could snap her with one arm. He didn't find that enticing, though. Instead, he opened her mouth wider with his fingers and then let his mouth cover them. He freed himself quickly from his trousers. He could hear her start to pray. "Que Dios nos ayude a usted y a mí." She said this over and over again, louder and louder each time.

He forced her to look at him and then demanded, "Kiss me."

She softened her gaze and closed her eyes. When he forced himself inside her, she took the scissors across his cheekbone and dug in as deeply as she could.

The police commissioner stared at Mr. Johnson as they sat in the middle of a large office. The man's desk was slathered in paperwork that would never be completed. Mr. Johnson kept a linen napkin pinned to the right side of his face; it had round circles of fresh, bright-red blood in several places.

"Did she come to you with a letter of reference?" the commissioner asked.

Johnson glared at the man so hard he thought to abandon the question. "Understand. These things happen, Mr. Johnson. Household staff—they are itinerants. Often they pick up and move without giving notice. But there are remedies."

Again, Johnson said nothing, as if the commissioner had not yet fully understood what this was all about. "There are ways to help you."

Johnson leaned in. "Two women have marked my life. One betrayed me. The other stabbed me with a pair of fucking scissors! The first paid with her life. I don't see why the other shouldn't meet the same fate."

"Mr. Johnson...that is a messy idea. There is a child. She was a possible witness to what occurred."

Johnson took a pouch from his coat pocket. Staring at the commissioner, he poured a bag of gold coins on the desk. The commissioner stared—then, slowly, his eyes looked directly into Mr. Johnson's. "Yes. I understand. The whore has to pay for what she did to you... the child, though...could create trouble, for all of us, if she stays here."

They paused, both refusing to speak. Then the commissioner said, "I don't ride my horse across the city killing innocents souls, Mr. Johnson. The woman will pay—I assure you—but the child will live. Will you arrange for the girl to go with you?"

"With me—where?"

"To where you will soon live again. North America. You can't stay here, not after what we will do. You'll have a room for the creature in your big house, I'm sure. Maybe, if you are kind enough, she will forget this ever happened. Truly, it solves so many problems all at once. Your problems. My problems. You understand, I hope."

Johnson thought about the proposal, stupid as it sounded. He took a new bag of gold and placed it on the desk.

The commissioner let the bead of sweat trickle along his upper lip. "You have to take the little girl with you, for me to agree. Send me a photograph. One for each new year. You can use that black box of yours. One each year, yes? And send it to me...then I will do as you ask."

Johnson stood, nodded in agreement, and left.

CHAPTER THIRTEEN

Sea Girt, New Jersey, 1890

By morning, Isabel and Joseph were tangled together on the floor. Neither was sure how they had landed there. The bedsheets cascaded off the mattress and pillows were strewn about the room. It didn't much matter to Joseph. He had never felt this way— nothing even close. It was an odd mix of spinning energy and complete peace. He had woken before Isabel, and he used the time to explore in the daylight what he had only felt with his hands the night before. This time he noticed the scars on her lower back and hips, the *cruelty at his father's treatment*; the words that Elizabeth mentioned to him five nights ago. They were now the beginning of hundreds of questions he didn't dare to ask, like:

Why hadn't Isabel said anything to him?

What crime had his father committed?

How much does she remember about what happened in Colombia?

Or does she just want to forget the past?

And maybe the most important question: What was the real reason he brought the child to New Jersey? It was obvious his father disliked her. Why did he bother bringing her to his own house?

Then it came to his mind the words his nurse told him once: "The past is the past, Joseph; if you let it use you, you will drown."

Isabel woke with soft sighs, which then grew in intensity each time he delved into soft folds with his lips, his fingers, his tongue.

When he was sure she was fully awake, he whispered, "I have seen you before."

"Yes? Where?"

"I think, maybe…in paintings. On the street, in London, maybe. In my dreams, possibly."

Her body shook with a small laugh. She was sure he was partly crazy. "A fairy tale, then? I knew it."

He turned and held her face so she was forced to look at him. "No," he said firmly. "This is real." He placed his hand on her heart and then on his own. "You're here. I'm here."

Joseph studied how her eyes narrowed. The tension ticked her jaw once, then twice. "You should not be scared of my father, Isabel. I will make sure this is all made right. I will talk to him— tonight, if you like, about us—"

"No!" She placed her fingers over his mouth, as if this might stop his feelings from surfacing. "We need to wait."

"Why?"

"You do not know him as I do."

"What are you scared of?"

"He will find a way to ruin everything. Everyone. I know this about him. You, me…Elizabeth. She is my friend, Joseph."

"None of what was supposed to happen between Elizabeth is turning out as it should. She knows that as well as I do."

"I am saying this again. Be quiet. We need to be careful. Very, very careful."

Joseph's mind ran backwards, to the letter at Dr. Edwards's place, to the cautious, distant father he barely knew. The questions swirled and interfered with all he felt.

"I will wait…but not for long, do you understand? I am not patient enough. One taste"—he let his teeth graze her ear—"and I am hooked."

She smiled, but did not answer him. Both were silent for a long time after that.

"I hated the tales with fairies Sarah used to tell me," she finally said.

"They always have happy endings."

"Horrifying monsters always stand in the way." Her eyes were like ribbons of the past. He wanted to grab and shake them out of her.

"No monsters in New Jersey," he said before he took her again. "I've checked."

◦◦◦

"Have you gone mad?" Sarah asked. She stood in the middle of the cabin; she had not even bothered to place her basket on the table.

Isabel went in and out of the room. She was changing her clothes, her face flushed, pinning her hair into submission as best she could. "Yes, utterly."

"And what about his father?" Sarah asked.

"What about him?" She sounded almost dismissive. It scared Sarah half to death.

"Don't you realize what Mr. Johnson might do?"

"Kill me, you mean? If he hasn't done it before, he won't do it now. Sarah…" She stopped once, her eyes shifting so that Sarah might understand what she was about to say. "There is a reason he keeps me here."

"I think you're gullible." Sarah was so upset now, frustrated; startled tears formed in her eyes. "You are miscalculating. I am sure of it."

"No, Sarah. I am not. I told you: things have changed. And for him, things are not working out as well as he might like."

Sarah sat in the one chair and then looked up at Isabel, pleading, "This will not break well, child. Take the chance. Leave. Be free."

"Leave?" Isabel was astounded that Sarah would even voice those words. "No. Not until he pays for his crime."

"This will ruin you both!" Sarah said. She put the basket on the table and left without another word. Isabel collapsed onto the chair, hot tears now forming in her eyes. She wiped them away, pretending moments like this did not even exist.

Joseph stood in the doorway of his father's study. The very thought of him entering made him sick. He worried his breakfast might come up without warning. "Sit down," his father commanded. Joseph did as he was told, without a word. He watched while his father moved about the room. At first there was no pattern; he seemed to be doing several things at once, none of them related to the other. But then he placed his hands on papers that lay across his desk and walked them over to his son. "Read them."

Joseph began to look through them. They were clearly formal legal papers, the language oblique and stilted, with watermarks from a notary and signatures that followed several clauses, all of them his father's. "What is this?" Joseph looked up at his father.

"Your future."

Joseph looked again, stunned by what he now read:

LARCHMONT RESIDENCE
18 CARRIAGE LANE
HAMPSTEAD
WEST LONDON NW 6 ENGLAND

He saw notations about the deed being transferred, followed by his formal name in capital letters: JOSEPH BROOK DODGE JOHNSON. NEW OWNER. "These are the deeds to the London house?" he asked.

His father nodded, "We are bootstrappers, us Johnsons," he said. "I didn't rise. I kicked—I bit—I clawed. And iron was the thing. Steel. Everyone needs it. Without it, without us, the northeast would be a backwater. The other factories—they didn't have the violence inside them. And when you don't want badly enough, you lose. One by one, I took them on. And one by one, they fell. Within a decade, before you could even stand, we were the single biggest factory. Never, not once, did I ever want for myself." He looked at his son. "It's why I have a fortune."

Elizabeth walked along the dunes. Her little brother, Thomas, just turned ten, chased gulls along the waves. She had let him come along, riding in front of her on the saddle, and drifted behind him now as she walked the horse, holding the reins loosely in her hand. She wasn't sure if she had meant to end up at the cabin. She didn't tell anyone where she was going, nor did she ask Thomas if that was where he wanted to go. Instead, she just gravitated there.

She had not seen Isabel in what felt like a lifetime. When her father told her about Isabel's diagnosis, she had cried herself to sleep, unsure how she could be without Isabel. She felt weak in a way she had never felt before. If every day was to be one where she was slighted—or worse, ignored—she was sure she would curl up and die.

She knew what tuberculosis meant. She had always listened at the table when her father talked of various illnesses, so she knew she was not supposed to be within Isabel's reach. But she longed for someone who looked at her and saw…somebody.

She had leaned against the wall the night before, outside her father's office, listening—to what, she was not sure. Her father's voice was tense, going from bravado to high soprano more than once. He was talking about Isabel; she finally made that out. Why? He hadn't spoken of her for years, nor had he ever allowed Elizabeth's mother to invite her to the house. He barely acknowledged that Isabel was alive. Isabel had only once seen the inside of Elizabeth's bedroom, but that was because Elizabeth had snuck her in on a rare day when both her parents had gone to New York. Had something happened to her? She waited to hear dreaded words or to catch a phrase about an undertaker, but none had come. All she heard in the end was her father saying, "This has gone far enough," and then, "Joseph is obsessed with her."

She paused then. Like lightning, it lit her brain. It was a fact she had not thought of…but it somehow made sense. All the conversations with Joseph were about Isabel, her past, her present, her future. *She is the woman he really cares about,* she thought. And somehow, she was okay with that.

She led the horse up the dunes to the cabin and let him feed on the sea grasses while she approached slowly. She wasn't sure if she should she call out. Surely, standing several feet away, in this brisk wind, her hat barely atop her head, it would be safe to talk. She had ordered Thomas to stay down at the beach; under no circumstances was he to come near Isabel. She was fairly sure he had listened to her; he was happy with the waves and the gulls, and his found walking stick kept him occupied.

Isabel came out, her hair wet from a washing. They stood apart, smiling for a long time, before Isabel sat atop the log outside the cabin. Elizabeth approached her, noticing how well she looked—and then said, her voice slightly shaky, "I wasn't sure I should come. If you would even let me…"

Isabel's look was her answer. "You can always come. You know that."

Elizabeth watched her friend closely. "You look—incredible? Is that the right word? I am so—"

"I am not sick, Elizabeth. I know it. It's a lie. You don't have to worry."

Elizabeth was not sure what that meant, but she walked over to Isabel. Elizabeth did not doubt anything Isabel had ever said, and it seemed, frankly, stupid to do it now.

"Oh, God. I am so relieved. So, so"—she grabbed Isabel in a hug before the younger girl could stand up properly—"relieved." She refused to let her go before they sat again.

Isabel looked down at where Thomas played. "I will marry that boy one day," she said with a mischievous smile. "He was meant for me, and me alone."

Elizabeth laughed. "Don't even joke, Isabel. If I told him that, he would wait only until the moment he came of age. You see how he freezes when he comes near you. No man knows what to do around you, Thomas included. You are far too beautiful."

Isabel looked at her in a way that confirmed what Elizabeth had heard the night before. Isabel didn't have to say a word. Elizabeth knew—something had happened.

"You can always come, and bring him," Isabel said.

"I'm sorry I haven't come before." She looked at her again, trying to say what she could not say openly. "The wedding has taken over all of our lives. My parents haven't left me alone for a minute." Isabel said nothing for a long while; she bowed her head, her feet tracing patterns in the sand.

"Isabel?" Elizabeth asked. "Am I right that we keep no secrets?" Isabel looked at her and nodded silently. Elizabeth seemed close to tears again.

Isabel lifted her hand to caress her cheek. "What is it? Tell me."

Elizabeth wiped a second tear quickly. "When we were young, you told me how Mr. Johnson took you away from your mother, your country...I wanted to say this then, and never did. I believe you, all the stories you told me back then. I believed every word. I always have."

Isabel shook slightly.

"Fear has conquered me all my life," she continued. "I have never had the courage you have." She let the words spill out before she could push them back in. It was why she was here—she knew it now. She had to show Isabel how weak she truly was. "This union, while not what I choose...if I am to—there is nothing in me that sees how it can turn right-side up if I refuse."

Elizabeth looked up to the sky and continued. "My neckline flatters. I am quick-witted. But that is all." She let a tear fall. "If you could see this in me, if you could understand that I am not you..."

Isabel looked into Elizabeth's eyes. "I did not ask him to come."

Elizabeth smiled. This was the best friendship she would ever have; that was so clear to her. "Of course not. I'm not stupid. You are irresistible."

Isabel looked away.

"Don't apologize," Elizabeth said quickly. "It's wonderful news that you experienced beauty. If I had been asked, I would say I would want you to have that." She placed her hand on Isabel's. "But leave it here." She went silent. "Please. Mr. Johnson did terrible things to you when you were a child, and I have no doubt he will do worse if he knows."

"I know that," Isabel said tersely.

"He must not find out...what you have done." She stood and called out for Thomas. "I have to go. I wasn't supposed to be doing

this. I wasn't supposed to be here…bridesmaids' dresses to hem…
which seems stupid now, doesn't it?"

Isabel barely raised her eyes.

"Don't do that, Isabel," Elizabeth said sternly. "We have always
been honest with each other. To stop now would be idiotic." She
pulled Isabel in and held her with a vise-like grip. "I love you as
I always have, and always will. Whatever happens, Isabel. I mean
that. Whatever happens. If Mr. Johnson and my father haven't
done anything against us by now, it's because no matter what, they
are sure they will have the last word, Isabel."

"But there is a way out for us—"

"No, Isabel. Don't swim against the tide; you will drown,"
Elizabeth interrupted, distressed.

"I have a plan, Elizabeth. I'm *sure* it will work." She affirmed *sure*.

Cartagena, Colombia, 1880

There were five of them; they all had rifles strapped to the front
of their bodies. The men stayed atop their horses until they were
deep inside La Boquilla, the fishermen's village. One by one they
dismounted, pulled their rifles, and cocked them at the ready while
roaming the lean-tos, the shaky huts, the tented open shanties.
They yelled loudly as they went, never wanting to ambush, but to
terrify and stun. Each man asked about a woman and a child.

Isabel appeared in the doorway of a hut. She clutched herself,
not knowing what to do. She looked back inside the darkness of the
empty clay room. All she could see were her mother's burning eyes.

"Go," her mother hissed. Isabel refused to move. "Go! Do what
I said."

"Yes, Mama," Isabel said, and then took off. Her bare feet were
sore; it hurt to walk, much less run, as they slapped across the stale,
infested puddles. She zigged and zagged, taking one row and then

another in no particular pattern, except that she moved in a deliberately messy way, off the harbor and up the sloping hill. She would go to the commissary and find a police officer to help them. Her mother had stashed a few bills inside her underwear in case something like this happened.

Isabel dodged, weaved, and doubled back once. Then, when she made a sharp turn to climb the stone streets that began Cartagena proper, where the fishermen's village ended and the ancient wall began, she ran straight into the legs of a man. A giant.

Margarita shook, holding herself as best she could. She could not think straight. She knew she needed to think, but no real thoughts came to her. Mr. Johnson had already broken her arm when she had escaped his house a few nights before. The arm now lay limp and useless at her side. She thought briefly about wading into the surf and swimming around the point until she reached the far side of town, but the tides were so high and she was too weak, one arm pulling her under the surf. She was sure she would be drowned— or worse, caught.

Then, she froze. She heard Isabel's cries. At first they were so thin, as if she were miles and miles away, but the cries grew louder, and when they did, Margarita pushed herself up the bed.

"Mama…Mama…Mama!"

"Isabel?" Margarita said, first as a whisper, then loudly, "Isabel!" She fell to the doorway and leaned in to listen again. She heard a man's voice, stern and even: "We have your girl."

She scanned the doorways, then slipped out, half-crouching, like an animal, looking for the sound of her daughter's voice. "She is a pretty one," the man's voice said. "I wonder how much she is worth?"

Margarita began to cry. "Let her go! Let her go!" She turned a corner and there the giant stood, with a smile plastered on his face.

Margarita refused to look at him. Instead, she gazed down at her daughter. "Isabel, *hija*," she said weakly.

The giant, Jacinto, was so large he had to duck under doorframes as he approached the commissioner's desk. The bottom half of Jacinto's trousers were caked in dust. The commissioner, one of two men left in the building at that hour, was squeezing a lemon zest into his glass of water, indifferent to the papers strewn across his desk. "Hello, Giant," he said softly.

"We have found who you are looking for," Jacinto said crisply. The commissioner sighed. Jacinto did the dirtiest work the commissioner had and did not push for cleaner work, for which the commissioner was grateful. He reluctantly pushed his body off his chair, took his coat, and followed the officer out the door.

The commissioner and Mr. Johnson entered the dark room an hour later. The commissioner turned the heavy lock with a key and let a sliver of moonlight into the blank room. Margarita leaned against the far wall. Her daughter leaned into her lap. Both women's hands were tied. She was soiled from head to toe and her hair was matted, slicked back with sweat and oil. Neither man said anything.

The commissioner smiled at Margarita, who went from being inconsolable to weeping openly. "Don't worry, we will take care of the small girl." He offered his hand to Isabel as if he were her father. "Come now, please. We have to conduct some business; then it will all be over. I promise."

Margarita stood, touching her daughter for last time, and stepped toward the man.

The commissioner left, carrying the desperate child, and then Mr. Johnson took his shirt off and approached the woman.

The Giant took Margarita's unconscious body out to the bay. She lay lifeless in the back of the open wagon, her scalp scarred, her eyes grayed, the jaw out of socket. She would not be able to utter a sound if by a miracle she began to breathe properly. Jacinto had not ever done a job like this before. He had never known the commissioner to ever have to ask such a thing.

He took the body to the sea. It was just before dawn. He stopped at the water's edge, then dismounted. He let go of the reins when he took Margarita's body into his arms. He carried her farther out to sea. First his legs were covered, and when he reached his chest, he let go and watched the body drift. It moved slowly. Her legs submerged first. Her soft, bare face was the last part to submerge below the waves.

PART THREE

PERFECT STORMS

CHAPTER FOURTEEN

Sea Girt, New Jersey, 1890

Joseph tried to find ways to survive the daylight hours when he was forced to stay away from Isabel. He thought he had a chance to remain sane, but it was completely impossible. After just one day, he was convinced he was certifiable.

She had left his bed that first morning, slipping away while he dozed. He woke, his hands searching for her even before his eyes had opened. He had just been with her, but he still needed her again, frantically. He was hot with anger those first moments. That she could leave him alone this way—how could she do that? He was in awe of her ability to control herself, for clearly he had none. He tried to calm himself; he needed to get a handle on what felt like a spiraling, chaotic desire, a love so out of control it leveled him. He told himself he should feel sated, having had her as many times as the nighttime hours allowed and as many times as she could withstand. At one point she had whispered desperately, "Enough. Enough. I cannot do more." This merely made his chest hurt with joy. All he did in response was to kiss her swollen lips with more hunger.

So why was he feeling like a hot wire, taut, boiled like a poker, easily severed? In one short night he had developed an affliction, an appetite that felt insatiable. He was strangely unable to speak, only willing to do one thing: find her again and have her.

His breath hitched. He had to tell himself to take in air as he clawed the sheets before pushing his body upright, shifting his fingers through his tousled hair. Then he cooled, having caught a hint of scents of sea spray and mint from her hair, which mingled among the sheets. He closed his eyes again and went for his clothes, his shirt still half off by the time he found his boots downstairs. He was out the door and in the barn a moment later.

He found her walking the tides, her bare feet slapping the water. She wore a chemise, for the day promised to be hot, and her skin was already tanning. Her hems were stained from the salt water. When he saw her, he should have eased, but he urged on the horse faster. He did not greet her once he had swung off the horse or ask why she had left his bed without waking him. Instead, he gripped her, pulling her tightly to him. "Wrap your legs around me," was all he could manage to say. She looked at him and was about to answer but somehow thought better of it. "Now, please," he said urgently. She then did as she was told. He lifted her easily and carried her back to the cabin.

There, he refused to move—or to allow her to be free. They stayed there, that way, touching, laughing, eating only when they had to, until nightfall.

As the sun fell, she woke him by letting her fingers drift across his brows. She barely touched his skin, but his eyes opened. He smiled as he listened to her soft inhales. They were like a child's. He looked at her for a long while, trying to discern what she was thinking. He had not done what he needed to do—he had not spoken to his father, nor stopped the wedding—and he could feel the weight of her feelings pushing him backward, like a vortex. "Have you seen Elizabeth?" he asked her finally.

"Yes. She's not just scared of Mr. Johnson and Dr. Edwards, but leaving her mother and her little brother…the possibility of not seeing them again, it's terrifying for her." They fell silent.

"I understand that," he said.

She gazed at him before speaking again. "You must not come here for several days. I won't let you come."

"Why?" he asked.

"Because this must be done right."

"What do you mean?"

"On the wedding day, you'll be in church, waiting for Elizabeth… but she will not come. In her absence, the wedding will have to be called off."

Joseph did not answer immediately. He suddenly could see the child in Isabel, her ability to boil life down to its simplest ideas, without strange half-truths, without awful, ugly contradictions. "I doubt it will be that easy, Isabel."

She rose, leaning her bare back against the stone wall behind the bed. "The guests will go back home. Those who are closest to your father will come to his house, and I'll be there, waiting for you to introduce me."

"I doubt that will work."

She had clearly not heard a word he had said. "That's the only way your father won't be able to do anything against us…in front of so many witnesses." She turned and saw the questions that lined his face. She moved to get up but he grabbed her wrist, pulling her back. Refusing to look at him this time, she buried her face below his neck.

"Why do I have to stay away until then?" he asked.

"You must know—know what you are doing," was all she said.

*

He survived this purgatory for five days and five nights after she had banished him—where nothing happened, where life stood stone-still—before he was convinced he would go mad. He was sure, for example, that the clocks had literally stopped ticking. He rose, ate breakfast, looked through books in the library, and watched as if he were a stranger while the house staff began the big preparations for the wedding.

While the stable boys moved large furniture pieces to make room for a larger dance floor, wooden crates filled with china were transported into the house. The gardeners were shaping the boughs of wisteria that hung over the two back pergolas. Glasses were polished one by one in the kitchen. But all this seemed to take only a heartbeat; when Joseph looked at the clock above the library mantel, the afternoon had not yet finished.

Joseph leaned inside the library door, watching his father work. "I am going to take a day or so and see New York," he said.

His father looked up at him, his face silent and stony.

"I saw nothing of the city when I arrived," Joseph continued, "and Elizabeth and I will be gone before I can explore the place."

His father looked down at his desk and then silently nodded.

Joseph was at Isabel's door soon after. A small overnight case was strapped to the back of his mare. His hands shook as he tapped the wooden door. When she refused to open, he leaned into the frame and said, "I know you told me I was not to come." He let the words sink into the wood frame of the door. "But I could not stay away...I couldn't." Tears formed against his lids as he let them close. "I need you, Isabel. Now. Tonight. Tomorrow. Always."

He began to feel his weight sink, but then the door opened and he smiled, if weakly. "If I'm going to introduce you as my princess, you will have to let me take you to New York so you can dress the part."

He loved the feel of her, her legs pinned against his, her back to his chest as they rode through the fog and onto the main roads that led onto the ferry that was taking them into New York Harbor. He was worried she would stiffen. The ride was long, and her body was pinned to his to stay warm. She was normally soft and pliant, and so to stay that way, often she would reach her arms back and wrap them around his body. Or, to tease him, she would flip herself around and face him, her legs wrapped against the small of his back, her tongue teasing his open neck. It was as if they were one body this way, breathing in and out as one, sensing as one.

Two worn tugboats made their way south toward the harbor. Joseph followed them with his eyes as the boats drifted downwind, where they would pick up the large ocean liners bound for Europe. He felt like tugging Isabel by the arm and yelling for the boats to stop, take them aboard, let them scramble up and onto a liner unnoticed, let them disappear into a new...world. He stopped himself—he wouldn't allow ways to play the game that was his future. He was too unsure of his opponent, how the moves would unfold. Also, he couldn't see a way for him and Isabel to come out the other end in one piece.

The warm rains had checked the dank humidity, and he should not have felt as chilled as he did. Her skin was hot to the touch, and it quieted the hammering of his heart for him to touch her lips with his fingers. "It is only another half-hour or so before we reach the city. Have you been, ever?" She shook her head no. "Good that I should be the one to show it to you first. That makes me happy. It's an elegant place. Lots to see."

The city's wide streets were empty, except for the odd street cartsman who had idled past the workday. Joseph bought meat pies and two bottles of beer from a cart, and they let the mare slow her gait to a crawl so Isabel could take in this new world. Buildings lined both sides of the street; Isabel could not stop staring at the endless stories, one floor atop the other, in large, imposing, square structures, one right after the other. It was a city of layers, made for secrets, she was sure of it. Anyone could bury themselves deep inside the alleys, the dark corners, and never be discovered; a deep maze it was, a place she felt safe.

Joseph offered his arm to her as they stopped in front of the Astor House Hotel. Liverymen dressed in formal coats took the mare at the entrance and allowed them both to waft inside the still hotel. Just one man stood on duty at the front desk at that hour. He made her nervous; his eyes were too close together, and he barely looked her way when Joseph asked him for a room.

"The length of stay, sir?" the deskman asked, his eyes pinned to a lone mosquito that buzzed above their heads.

"I am not sure," Joseph said after a moment. "A few days at most."

The deskman glanced at Isabel's dark skin. His gaze did not move for several seconds. Joseph placed his hand on the front desk, tapping his fingers once or twice, then placed several large bills on it. Soon the man began to offer a few vacant rooms. Isabel refused to look back as Joseph took her arm and led her to the electric lift. Only when they were high off the hotel floor did she dare look past the iron bars and down below. The deskman, his eyes up, were pinned on her, as if he knew of a terrible hidden truth. It made her shake some, and soon, defenseless, she looked away.

Windows lined each wall of the room, opening it to the city. Each window was large enough for three people to stand against its frame—or jump through it. The night sky was a silvery hue. Joseph and Isabel could hear the odd clap of horses' hooves on the street below. She went straight to the windows and stood there for the longest time, looking out. He had carried their things into the room and went about setting the cases down and turning down the bed before coming back and standing behind her. He could feel her shake slightly, and he held her shoulders. Then, more boldly, he wrapped his arms around her. He felt the salt of her tears drip down his arm and he turned her around to face him.

"Why are you crying?"

"I'm not completely sure," she said, bowing her head. Her behavior embarrassed her. He took his hand and guided her chin so she would look him in the eyes.

"Tell me...you can tell me anything."

"I am as scared as I am happy, I think." She wasn't sure if that was even the right answer, but it helped to get something out. It felt as if part of a dam had broken. "Will the man at the desk call the police?" she asked.

"No, of course not. Why do you think that?"

"He looked at me...as if..."

"As if what, Isabel?"

"It's impossible for you to understand."

"Then help me."

"People here...everywhere, really...they look at me...and they form a story in their heads about who I am, what I believe in, who I'll be. They know nothing, of course. But they're so very sure."

Joseph took a strand of loose hair and tucked it behind her ear. "No more tears," he said, as if it were a command. "Show me a smile. The future lies inside your heart. Not in theirs." He touched her lips with his fingers, grazing them back and forth a few times before he kissed her. "Are you ready for bed? You must be exhausted."

She let him dry one more tear, and then she smiled. Before he could take her hand she walked to the bed, peeling away clothes piece by piece. By the time she had reached the bedframe, he offered her the box he had stashed underneath it when they had

arrived. When she opened it, the tiara was there. "You are my princess," he said softly to her.

❧

Sarah glanced toward Mr. Johnson. He had finished shaving and
was doing his tie. He looked up when she called after him, "Excuse
me, sir. Will you be here for supper?"

"No," he said. "The Edwards have asked me for supper. I have to
go to the church, pay the minister, and arrange for a few last things
before that. I will be at the ironworks during the day if you need me."

"Very good," she said in her clipped way. She waited for him
as she always did when it looked as if he might pass her in the hall;
deferring to him was a clue to the harmony that existed between
them. She let him lead her down the stairs, and there they parted—
he to the front door, she to the kitchen.

He took his time ambling down the gravel road to town. He
had filled his head with lists most every day of his life, and today
they were about flowers and guests, space allocated for the reception, the passages he had booked for Joseph and Elizabeth for their
return to London, and finally, the settlement of affairs at the ironworks before the governor arrived for the wedding. The governor's
assistant, an officious young man with a sharp tongue, had made
it clear to Johnson that all affairs with the iron factory had to be
resolved for the governor to accept his invitation. "He does not
associate if it presents a risk," the assistant had written to Johnson.

The list of concerns all blended together. He was relieved
when he thought about his son leaving. He had never been sure
he was the boy's true biological father—his mother made sure his
doubts remained active until her death. He should have resolved
this somehow, but he never found the time, and it never seemed
particularly important; Joseph was more a name than a son. He
had no emotional space inside him for a boy, or a man, even if it

were his own—any family, for that matter. These past two weeks had proven that. He preferred his solitary life, particularly since being in the same room with the son of that woman made his veins feel brittle and cold. Her seductive scents were always in his nostrils and he could feel her sometimes, just behind him, whispering terrible, empty threats.

Joseph's mother had hated him more than any woman he had ever come across, and his conquest of her was a proud moment. She bit him once, hard, on the ear after a fight about Joseph's lineage. He yelled like a dog, certain she had taken the lobe off. He was so consumed with relief when he saw her dead, her body white as a sheet, her neck purpled by his calloused fingers, her lifeless eyes looking back over his shoulder—thinking, stupidly, that he might have let her go free. *No*, he confirmed to himself, *Joseph is best placed out of sight, out of mind.*

Johnson slowed the cart at the sight of one of the new crank-start vehicles stalled by the side of the road. The passengers, a young couple and their daughter, looked up as he passed. The young girl, six or seven at most, was in front of the car, half on her knees, trying to help her father turn the crank, allowing the engine to spring to life. The mother, no more than thirty, stood beside them.

Johnson's eyes met with those of the young girl, and while there was a moment when he was sure he was looking at Isabel ten years earlier, he shook the flawed notion out of his head. The couple stood, certain Mr. Johnson would stop and lend them assistance. Instead he passed by, his eyes still pinned on the girl, his face impassive, almost imperceptibly threatening.

"Isabel," they heard him say under his breath.

He slowed the horse, thought a moment, and dug his knees into the horse's shoulder so that it would make the slow, wide turn that would lead to Isabel's cabin.

He circled the cabin more than once, peering inside the windows and making note of all he saw. It was not a home, but he knew it was Isabel's instantly. Her presence screamed throughout the small rooms: the flowers he had always smelled when he passed her old bedroom, the books—she had been an unapologetic thief from the time she had arrived at the house, and seeing his stolen books did not surprise him in the least. He spied her bed. The sheets were twisted; she had not made any attempt to tidy up. Then he stopped, leaned in to see closer, took off his hat, turned the corner to enter, and stood by the open bedroom door.

The painting leaned against the wall, next to the bed. He bent down to see it at eye level.

His eyes narrowed. He began to reel back, his head tilted back, and his eyes closed as each event of the last few weeks unfolded: Joseph's trips to the Edwards' house, the caustic meeting with the doctor about Isabel, and Joseph's persistent, nosy questions…*This is why he has been down here…Isabel.*

There were many moments when he thought it easiest to rid himself of her. She annoyed him on the best of days, which was enough excuse for him, and it would have been easy to do. Whenever she was openly defiant, he would see the rims of her eyes turn blood red the way her mother's had, and he entertained the possibility that she would come one night and slit his throat in his sleep. Those days he woke, certain it would be best for him to bury the child in a grave somewhere, but he never did it. He thought once or twice about why it amused him. There was the letter, and the photographs the commissioner had demanded as proof of life, photographs he'd sent for three years running. When he didn't hear from the commissioner again, he stopped—grateful, happy, even. *Such a stupid man, that commissioner. He'll surely come to a stupid end. Dead,* he hoped.

But there were other obstacles: Edwards and his idle, idiotic threats that came to nothing but still put him on edge. There was the idea he could possibly have both the mother and the daughter one day; all he had to do was wait for her to be of a certain age, and then…it had felt like a conquest worth waiting for. This thought aroused him. He never cared much about what excited his sexual interest; be it blood or a forceful, violent encounter, it made little difference to him, as long as it ended in his own pleasure.

He stood up, tearing the painting with his knife, ripping the frame back and forth until it split the canvas in two. His hand slipped and sliced a small section off his palm. He grabbed a kerchief of Isabel's and staunched the wound quickly, then stood to go.

No matter, he thought as he left the cabin. He left the door wide open so it would be clear he had been there. He would always make sure mistakes never caught up to him. They never had before; why would they now?

CHAPTER

FIFTEEN

New York

The two had trouble getting out of bed. Joseph would not let her move from the mattress; all she had to do was roll over onto her side, and Joseph pulled her back into his chest, nipping at her neck. His teeth sometimes took hold of her, pulling her toward him that way, which always brought up a small rumble of laughter in her. She did this silently—a soft, subtle rocking of her ribs that went straight to Joseph's heart. He was learning how she moved, the secret parts to her no other man had ever seen or known. It did not calm his nerves—it set them on fire. He was more possessive, needy of her in ways he had never known. He elicited quiet yet urgent pleas when he felt her back arch, when her neck rose and she fell, helpless for a moment, allowing him complete control of her.

"Yessss," he would say in soft pleas. "I love it when you fold into me like that…more." She rarely ever spoke while they were entwined; she answered only with sighs and an utter willingness.

She let him do whatever he wanted with her. It was why he could not let go of her, even now, when he could have her again and again.

They left the room only to satisfy their hunger. He took her out for a late supper. Then they went to two, three boisterous halls, filled with spilled beer and crushed peanuts, the loud catcalls of longshoremen ringing as he and Isabel moved about the dance floor. She felt like water when they danced; she placed her hands around the small of his back so he would feel more at ease. He was all legs and arms and had none of her grace, but with her, he moved naturally. She told him not to look down at his feet, but to watch her eyes. Grateful for this counsel, he found his rhythms.

They walked the full length of the island from the southeastern edge, where she stared blankly at the Statue of Liberty for the longest time, wiping tears away at the end. They walked along the broad avenues that took them past the parks and carriages and up to the dark clubs scattered uptown. They ate rice made with coconut water and fried shrimp, meals she had not experienced since childhood. They laughed at each other's stupid jokes. He bought her a red dress he paid for quickly when she modeled it for him. Then he took her back to bed, where they slept little and twisted and turned in the sheets like wild children.

The second day, he made her sit before a medical specialist while the doctor poked and prodded, asking question after question. Isabel glared at Joseph angrily throughout the entire visit, but it was worth it to him to hear the doctor declare her healthy and fit in the end. She would not speak to him for a full two hours after; for part of that time she walked four lengths in front of him, never looking back once. It was only when he broke down, twisted her to face him and kissed her, hard, without any warning, without permission, that she slapped him across the cheek and said, "I told you I was well. You should have just trusted me." After that, she smiled again.

They ate fried fish at a small restaurant near the fishmonger's market at the very end of the island. When they finished, he looked at her and told her they had to go back to Sea Girt. She did not answer or ask why. Instead, she looked at him for a long time.

"Tell me what you are thinking," he said.

"I am looking for clues, ways to see inside your head, to know what kind of person you are."

"I am a man…in trouble," he said simply. "Deeply in love. I am wrecked."

She saw tears form at the edges of his eyes. Then, before she could think about what he had just said, a tear fell down his cheek. He wiped it away quickly, embarrassed to be looking this way. "It's a terrifying feeling, to be honest. I just hope I can survive." His smile was so pained that she did not push more. He took her by the hand and led her back to the Astor in silence.

When they reached the hotel and the mare was saddled, she let him lift her up. When he slipped in behind her, she reached behind, wrapped her hands around the back of his neck, and pulled him into her. His kissed her back, and then they began their way home.

It was just before a new moon, so little light existed. Joseph took care of the mare himself and made his way back to the cabin. Upon entering, they found the ripped painting. He made sure Isabel understood that from here on they both must be careful. The painting made Joseph's stomach turn. He gripped Isabel before he left her and told her to sleep with the rifle next to her bed, but Isabel knew better: She had to disappear until the wedding day. Before Joseph said another word, she was already thinking about twenty places where she could easily hide.

Joseph let his eyes adjust to the darkness before he could navigate the path toward the back door to the kitchen.

Before he reached the door, he heard a rustle—nothing more. But he stopped. He turned and looked about him. He could see nothing but the fluid shadows of the trees. He had his hand on the doorknob when a thin voice pierced the air. "I don't understand love," he heard his father say.

Joseph turned and saw him leaning into the oak tree's darkest shadow. He had apparently come from the orchards. "It has no point, as far as I can see," he continued.

As Joseph approached his father, he raised his hand as if to say, *Not another step.* Joseph stopped again, collected his thoughts, and then looked up. "Let me explain—"

"Nothing to explain," his father said calmly.

"Yes, there is. I did not mean for anything to happen—I did not plan this—"

"I couldn't care less what you have to say, Joseph. Truly."

Joseph watched the man as he approached the back door. "She means nothing to me, Father. It was a dalliance. Wild oats."

In that instant, Samuel Johnson felt something that connected the two of them for first time since Joseph arrived from England. He looked up and smiled a smile that was part amusement, part mischief. Joseph kept talking, this time faster. "Haven't you ever had a need for a taste of the other? The strange and rare?" He paused and then said, "Do you really think I'd give up the life you are offering me with Elizabeth for a woman like Isabel?"

His father came as close to his son as he had ever been. Their faces were inches from each other. Joseph met his gaze. He stuck both hands in his pockets to be sure his father did not see them shaking. "Smart," was all his father said in the end. Joseph didn't notice his father's bloody hand wrapped with a cloth.

The man opened the back door and was about to go in when Joseph added hastily, "Can you find a way to release her? After, I mean…it would be less awkward."

Samuel Johnson did not turn around, but Joseph heard him say, "Yes, Joseph, of course." Joseph let out stale, hot air from his lungs and then followed him in. He paused inside. He could use a shot of Sarah's whiskey, but then dismissed the need and went upstairs to bed.

Had he fulfilled this sudden desire, things might have changed. For he would have found Sarah inside the pantry, making room on the shelves for the incoming food. She was snuffing out her candle when she heard the men's voices. She clutched her middle until she thought it safe to move about again, but she had forgotten her tasks—all she wanted to do now was run.

Sarah was up long before the rest of the house the next day. She hurried down to the cabin and banged on the wooden door until Isabel appeared. The winds were undependable that day, shifting from east to west and then back again, twisting hair into the sky. They took Sarah's hat off her head twice. The shutters on the cabin windows flapped like batwings. The frantic sounds they made filled the air, making both women jump. Sarah clasped Isabel's shoulders with her strong hands. She yelled the words, but Isabel acted at first as if she didn't hear her. Sarah repeated what she had said and Isabel shook her head vigorously, as if the woman had lost her mind.

Finally, Isabel broke free of her, raised her arms up, and yelled, "No!" and, "Stop talking!" She plugged her ears in a vain attempt to wall out the words. "You are lying to me!" she screamed.

Sarah could only be heard to say the word *"Run!"* but it was possible, between the winds and the angry shutters, that she had said nothing at all.

Sarah gave up after a spell and headed back toward the house. She turned around after several yards, but Isabel was nowhere to be found.

CHAPTER
SIXTEEN

Without knowing it, both the bride and groom began to dress for the wedding at the exact same time. Joseph was fitted for his jacket. The tailor who had come first thing was not pleased with how the sleeves fell. He also wanted the pant cuff to break better on the shoe. So there were a few hours taken up before Joseph could call the suit finished. Elizabeth's dress, however, was a perfect fit from the moment she put it on. No one saw the need to move even a stitch.

The two men, Joseph and his father, left the house together. They truly looked like father and son. The younger, his step just as deliberate as his father's, followed closely behind. They had decided, on this beautiful day, to walk the ten minutes to church.

Sarah was still dressing when the two men left the house. She had been walking the length of the place, going over the table settings again and again, straightening knives that were askew, wiping glasses on her apron. Beyond the pergola she saw the liverymen uncorking wines, placing them in iced bins set in neat rows along the orchard edge. They had made a new gravel road so carriages could park behind the house and circle round to the front when called. They had expected at least twenty carriages. Those who arrived on horseback would make up the rest of the wedding party. Nearly one hundred people in all would arrive by sunset.

Sarah promised herself she would not soil her dress with sweat or grimy handprints. She had planned to fix her hair in a twist, and had let her thick hair down to braid it when she saw a figure pass behind her, moving down the length of the hall. She turned and went to her doorway, catching Isabel rounding the hall toward Joseph's room.

"Lord, child!" Sarah said, hurrying after Isabel. She turned the corner just as Isabel was opening Joseph's door, but she had closed it behind her by the time Sarah reached it.

She pushed the door open. Isabel was at the window, her hands wrapped tightly around a brown paper package. "He loves me." Her eyes were wild with fury, the rims swollen and red from crying. Her abdomen lurched and retracted as if she might throw up her insides any second.

"You cannot be seen here." Sarah tried to sound commanding, but it came out like a plea.

Isabel did not hear her. "You'll see," she said, her head shaking, her eyes pinned not on Sarah but on the ceiling above them.

Sarah tried to approach her, but Isabel panicked and backed up so quickly she hit her head against the far wall. "Isabel," Sarah said gently. "Men are cruel by nature."

Isabel was silent for a moment. "Not Joseph." Her gaze was accusing. Seeing that Isabel no longer believed her, Sarah was certain the poor girl had lost all sense of reason. Sarah's eyes went dull and flat as she looked at Isabel, feeling nothing but pity. No one had told her what happened to women, how life unfolded, so here now was the moment.

"*All* men, Isabel." She said this clearly so the words would puncture the girl's brain. Sarah refused to go on until Isabel looked her squarely in the eyes. "You are not perfect, God knows," Sarah continued. "But cruel you have not been. If you are to survive this, it will be because you do not give in to that. That you find a way to be what these men are not. Now go, and I will come for you when I can. I left you money in the basket. It will take you to New York, and I will see you there when I can and we can decide what to do after that." Then she whispered, "Go. Before it's too late."

Isabel allowed her to come close now. She was shaking uncontrollably. She didn't try to catch the tears that ran down her cheeks in rivers. Sarah took her by the shoulders, as she had done outside the cabin earlier, and leaned in to hug her, but Isabel pulled away suddenly. "No!" she hissed, then backed away. "Don't touch me! Or I promise I will bite you!"

The words scared Sarah to death. She backed away, bumping into furniture as she went, and closed the door behind her.

⁄⁀

Elizabeth had quietly locked her door after her mother, the last to leave, had finished doing her hair. She sat on the edge of her bed, her head dropped like a rag doll's. She felt strange, as if she weren't actually herself. She felt none of the things she had believed a day like this would bring—neither eagerness, nor fear. She felt…nothing, as if watching herself from afar, just waiting for things to happen.

"Elizabeth! Open the door!"

She jumped at the sound of her father's voice. He had been banging on her door for minutes before she finally noticed.

"I know what are you doing!"

She stood up suddenly at his screams. He had always treated her like a dense creature; now it was obvious.

"You knew about Joseph's true feelings for Isabel!" Tears began to fall against her cheeks.

Her father against the door, highly irritated, kept knocking. "You're not a little girl anymore, Elizabeth. So I'll be very explicit with you. Isabel and women like her are just pure entertainment for those young men like Joseph. Isabel was just his toy! If you know what I mean."

Elizabeth covered her mouth in disbelief. That was not true. She knew that. Didn't she?

"Joseph is a good man, offering you a family, a house, a fortune! You are the woman he wants to marry. Don't be silly. That's all that counts!

She waited for him to finish but he said nothing more for a couple minutes, and that silence scared her even more.

"Let me put it this way," he said. "After today, you are on your own."

"What? What do you mean?"

He clipped his words. "You can go to church or not, but I want you out of this house today!" He turned to go. "Let's get this over with, yes?"

The chapel fit just fewer than one hundred people, and most of those who were invited to the ceremony had filled the pews by now, sitting uncomfortably for just over an hour. Mr. Johnson had gone outside twice: once to look for signs of the Edwards, the second time to send Ben to their house to ask about the delay. When he came back in, the governor was at his side. He offered the governor and his wife seats toward the front and then made his way to the first pew, where a seat had remained empty for him.

Joseph stood exactly where his father had left him. He looked at no one, but stared out the etched windows, watching the horses idle outside.

A moment later, he felt a presence behind him. Elizabeth appeared. It was almost impossible to see her properly; her veil was covered in intricate designs. He could only catch hints of her eyes—glassy, unfocussed. Her cheeks were leaden but had a flushed peak, as if she had a low fever. She seemed shaky, even weak.

Mr. Johnson patted her shoulder indifferently and then walked up the aisle to meet his son. He nodded to the small orchestra, who began to play a summer wedding march.

Joseph looked up and saw Elizabeth walking unsteadily toward him. His whole body twisted and torqued. It hurt to take in air; a fierce headache struck his temple. Elizabeth did not have far to walk but she faltered twice, so her father held her up by gripping her elbow. She did not look at any one, including her fiancé. Her eyes were pinned to the stone floor as she approached the altar.

When she arrived, her father did not immediately step back. He indicated that Joseph needed to hold her steady because she would not be able to stand on her own. Joseph stepped in, took her hands and held them firmly. Then, when able, she looked up into his eyes. He smiled kindly—not the way a husband might, but she didn't expect him to.

Just as the minister moved in, Joseph held his hand up to stop him. Then he leaned in and whispered in Elizabeth's ear, "You know I can't do this, don't you?"

Her eyes turned from pale blue to a dark purplish gray. She let go of his hands as she stiffened and stepped back, stumbling as she did. He moved off the altar. "You should not want this, either," he said bluntly. "Say so. Tell the truth, if only to yourself."

He turned back to those who lined the pews. He thought to make a speech, but he knew it was not worth it, nor did he believe any of them would understand any of it. He turned and walked down the aisle. Samuel Johnson stood, dumfounded. He looked briefly at Dr. Edwards, then at the faces—the dazed looks, the barely concealed smirks, a few hiding wicked smiles in handkerchiefs. The filthiest to him were the faces lined with pity. *Pity?* It was revolting, the idea.

With that he waved his arms and roared like a wounded bear. A few were so scared off by the violent noise they stood from their seats. But his fists turned toward them instantly. "Stay where you are!" he ordered. They immediately fell in line, falling like rocks onto the hard pews.

Then he saw Sarah. She was standing behind the last pew, gripping its back so hard he was sure she would snap a plank of wood off in her hands. She was clearly frightened to death, as she ought to have been. He could snap her neck right now; one swift screw of his wrists, and she would be gone. Pure venom raced through his veins. He walked down the aisle, then stopped. "I will be back momentarily," he announced to the guests. "My son… he has lost his senses…clearly. I'm sure he understands what that might mean." And then he was out the door of the church.

Joseph had taken the first horse he could find—one of the livery boy's mares. He knew her to be frisky but fast on her feet. He was half a mile from the church when he felt a gnarled pain in his neck. He looked back and saw the vague outline, his father's large frame, bent over the neck of his horse, as if he were at the track. His speed must have been tremendous, for he was gaining on him quickly.

Joseph ground his heels into the mare. She bucked twice, twisting them both right, then left, before she could straighten her path and speed forward. He looked back; his father was closer. Joseph spurred the mare twice again, but it did no good.

Suddenly, he pulled upright. He was running from the man. It sickened him, the idea that cowardice could rise in him this way. The mare was racing at her fastest, so he leaned in and coaxed her several times to slow, and then he pulled her into circles, softening her gait so he could meet his father head-on.

The man was there a moment later. His eyes were black, his knuckles inflamed by the grip he held on the reins. He was white as a ghost, looking like a specter, a ghoulish vision come to take the air from his lungs and the sight from his eyes. The horses circled while the two men eyed each other. Joseph was waiting for the threats to explode, but instead, suddenly, his father grasped the reins. Joseph was pulled violently in and before he could resist, his father's hand was around his neck. It felt like a claw, not a human hand at all—the fingers punctured his larynx. Joseph's eyes bulged in pain.

"You will turn around *now!*" his father shouted. "Do you understand me?"

Joseph could only choke out a garbled, "No!" before he used his entire weight and threw his fist across and into his father's jaw. It punched the man back far enough to loosen his grip, and Joseph tugged his mare backwards. "I love her!" he shouted, spitting blood onto the dust below. Then he stared his father down. "I know why you want me to marry Elizabeth; the letter, the blackmailing—"

"You can't be *that* stupid, can you?" Samuel Johnson retorted. "Don't you know what I will do to you? Isn't it obvious to you?" He charged Joseph right then, grabbing the agitated mare with his bare hands this time. The mare groped back and bucked Joseph so hard it took all his strength to stay atop the saddle.

Joseph laughed. "What have you done, old man? Killed women? You have reached too far down into the devil's hole and you cannot get yourself out. And it won't be *me* who will help you. If we are trying to understand each other—here and now, in this moment—you need to know that."

His father smiled and pulled a piece of fabric from his trousers pocket. It had the rusted scents of dried blood, but the stains did not seem old at all. He offered it to his son. Joseph stared at it for a long time before taking it, looking up at his father only when he was sure the linen was hers. It certainly smelled like her—the sea air was in the fabric, her skin radiated off the blood.

"You have done something to her?" His voice cracked. It took all he had to say those few words. "Is that why you're showing this to me?"

The father held his son's gaze the whole time. He did not blink, nor did he flinch. He could wait as long as it took. Soon the boy would falter, he figured—he had taken from his son the only thing he had wanted, and that was enough.

Soon Joseph began to flinch. "You expect me to actually believe you? Now? After all your lying?"

"It's torn—from her dress, Joseph. The blood, it came from your little whore—"

"*Stop!*" Joseph screamed. "If any of what you say…any of it… that you touched her —that you even went *near* her, I swear—"

The man opened his mouth and pointed to his lips. "She tasted good, Joseph. She will again when I'm ready to have her once more."

Joseph's madness was silent…volcanic. He let go of his reins, and while the mare circled idly he let his head roll back to the sky, his hands covering his eyes.

His father turned his horse and began the path back to the church. He looked back. He had broken the boy utterly. "Back to the church, then," he said.

After a moment, Joseph turned the mare around and followed the man back.

CHAPTER SEVENTEEN

The ceremony took all of five minutes. Both Elizabeth and Joseph repeated the minister's words in flat phrases. Neither looked at the other, and when it was time to seal the vows with a kiss, Joseph eyed Elizabeth with such sorrow she could not help but let out an anguished groan. He touched her lips briefly with his own. His hands were wooden and stark as he walked her down the aisle.

Isabel sat in a chair in Joseph's room. She had emptied her head, she had nothing rolling around inside, she felt barely alive…nothing would happen, the wind would not move, the sun would not fall, nothing would occur until she saw him again.

She heard the footsteps stop before the door. She sat up, her breath caught in a fishnet. Then it opened and Sarah stood there, her face ashen and bleak. Isabel knew before she said anything aloud. Her head dropped into her hands, then her body followed, and she collapsed onto her knees.

"He just married Elizabeth," Sarah said softly. Then, as she closed the door, "I will pack your things after the reception and find you a horse."

✑

The ballroom was difficult to navigate. So many people filled the room, spilling out various open doors, onto the back, across the sides of the house. Many remained in the foyer. The servants wove throughout the open veins that were allowed them passage, and champagne glasses were in everyone's hands. Music wafted throughout the rooms, but every so often a guest, already under the spell of good whiskey and wine, would start an Irish ballad, and several of the men could be heard chiming in.

Heinous laughter came out in spurts, but it was not a lively, free sound. This party did not feel like a celebration, but more like a collective gathering of need, where desires were released, buttocks pinched, kisses stolen on the dance floor. No one was going to miss this Johnson wedding, if for no other reason than the mere spectacle of the thing.

Yet no one was here to share the joys, for they knew enough to be sure there were none. The music, the waltzes, were only for those who knew how to move about the floor in strict circles to formal, dirge-like rhythms. The others were lined up against the walls, pinning their champagne glasses to their chests, gossiping and whispering about what happened in church minutes earlier.

✑

In the library, Mr. Johnson stood before the governor. The politician was as wide as he was tall, and he had the habit of choking anyone in the room with his cigar smoke. The man's eyes drooped from too many backroom deals. His voice was a grinding mix of tension and threat. He listened, seated in Johnson's chair behind his desk. He had not asked permission to sit there, but when he took the seat, Johnson did not protest, for he knew without being asked what the man was here for—certainly not a wedding. Johnson told him of the ironworks negotiations, emphasizing the weaknesses in the workers' arguments, leaving out key areas that would cause the governor unease.

After several minutes, the governor stood up. "So if they gather to unionize, you are telling me you will break them. Is that accurate?"

Johnson nodded his head. "Yes. It won't be necessary—"

"I doubt that, Samuel. You run a sweatshop."

"They will comply with me. I have never lost a fight in my life. But I also have replacement workers at the ready if needed."

The governor looked hard at him. "Yes, I'm sure."

Samuel opened his mouth to a thin smile. "All is well. Let's go out and have something to drink."

When they reached the ballroom, the crowd parted for the two men. Many gathered like bees for a chance of a lifetime to be with the governor. He moved like molasses through the swarm, offering both his hands to anyone in immediate reach, stopping longer for those he knew or needed to know, passing those of no importance to him.

Johnson, however, bulleted his way through the party, rarely stopping at all. He knew everyone and had personally overseen the invitation list, but there was no one he cared to speak to. He took a glass of whiskey, then a second, and stood by the open doors, watching his son move about the room. Joseph's face was blank—it was impossible to read any life in it—but he was polite, stopping to listen as young men approached him. He nodded silently as men introduced themselves. He did not leave the room, pausing to take drinks when offered. Samuel saw him stumble once, certain his son had had several drinks by now.

Joseph looked at Elizabeth, who was taken apart from him by other young women, when he felt a pull on his elbow. Someone had gripped him from behind, possibly to break his fall. He stopped, annoyed, and was about to pull himself away when he saw Sarah, her face tear-stained, her shoulders stooped. She looked…heartbroken. He pulled away quickly, unable to survive any serious interrogation if she tried.

"It was necessary, Sarah," he said in a low whisper.

"What was, sir?" she asked.

"What I did. I had no choice—"

Sarah's look was so very confused. He fought past the fog the whiskey had caused. "I am fairly sure he killed my mother," he said. "I had to stop it—stop him."

"I don't know what you're talking about."

He was sure he was going mad now. The room began spinning, and he needed to find his way to a sink. He gripped her and leaned in so she would hear every word he uttered. "He's hurt Isabel, Sarah. He has her." His eyes welled with tears; they dropped carelessly on his suit.

Clearly, she was frightened; her voice sounded shattered and small. Despite that, she looked him squarely in the eyes and said, "Isabel is upstairs, in your room, sir."

He suddenly let her go. He had never felt so weak in his life. He began to move, but murmurs grew into small gasps, and then roars, and heads were turning. He pushed his way toward the stairs, but the tide of bodies was so dense it pushed him back. He forced his shoulders in, not caring whom he would elbow. Reaching the foyer, he stopped upon hearing his father's thin-veined, shrill voice: "Move out of the fucking way!"

Joseph looked up. Isabel was halfway past the landing, wearing the red gown he had bought for her in New York. It wrapped her waist tightly and draped over her hips and legs, falling just above the ankle. The tiara tilted slightly to one side of her head. She walked like a tin doll, with none of her fluid motion. She looked… mechanical. He fought to get near her, but she had pushed her way into the ballroom. By the time he had circled back, she was standing before his father and Elizabeth was gone.

Isabel smiled at the governor, who offered his professional greeting. She kept her biggest smile for Mr. Johnson, who took her by the elbow. She wriggled out of his grasp, more than once, and he yelled fiercely in her ear, "*Get out!*"

"Why? I live here," she said simply, jumping back to avoid him one more time.

Johnson looked at two house staff and ordered, "Get her out of here. Now!"

When the men placed their trays down and moved toward her, she raised her arms above her head. "What, will you kill me now? The way you did my mother?"

The governor looked up from his conversation, his brows knitted together. Johnson crowed loudly, "She is unstable! Ill in the head! I am looking for ways to help her, but she must be kept away from people…she is dangerous! Best to stand away from her!"

"You are *lying!*" she yelled. Her cheeks flushed red and she flung herself toward him. When he laughed, looking flushed, waxed, and polished, she grew feral. Before he could stop her, she slipped a knife out of her waist and sliced his face from eye to jaw—a long, thick line down his unflawed cheekbone.

Johnson wrapped his thick fingers around her neck and paused a moment, figuring he could push in hard and stop her breath within a moment or so. *It'll be easy,* he thought. *One moment she'll be here, the next…*but then the people around him. *Get the stupid piece of paper…then feel the thrall that'll come beneath my hands once I kill her.*

Suddenly, he felt his body torque backwards. His muscles tore loose as Joseph's knuckles slammed into the deep sockets under his eyes. Blinded, he let loose his grip and fell back. He lost his balance as Joseph slammed his fists once, twice, three times into his father's jaw and eyes. The bones cracked loudly in Joseph's ears as his father passed out.

The room was like a tomb, strangely. His son gripped Isabel by the waist and pulled her back against the wall of people until a crack in the wall appeared and the crowd swallowed them both up. No one thought to move. Then Joseph looked at the governor and said wryly, "What family doesn't have its ups and downs?"

The governor looked at him, then turned his back on the scene.

Isabel wrestled out of Joseph's grip. He lost sight of her once and then found her again, just as she was about to slip out the door. "Stop!" he ordered. But she didn't care what he said; the idea of him touching her was intolerable. She felt him at her back and then she whipped around, lashing the knife as she did. He jumped back as the blade ripped his waistcoat. He felt the blade score his stomach. "You have to listen to me," he pleaded. "He told me you were in danger. He showed me proof!"

She grabbed his head and pulled it into her and then bore her eyes into his. There was love in them—just a vicious, frenzied sort of love. She felt strong enough to choke him. "Do it," he said, reading her thoughts. "I'd be grateful at this point."

She released her hands, wanting to stop everything—the earth, the rains, the days, all of it. She dropped the knife and the tiara at his feet and ran.

CHAPTER EIGHTEEN

Isabel's knuckles scraped against the stone walls of the cabin until they were bloodied and bruised. She paced the floor back and forth, wearing a groove into the floorboards, stopping only when she heard her mother's voice. She had first heard her calling when she had arrived. She had started to throw what possessions she had in a rucksack but had stopped, screamed, and swept everything off the tables around her. She stilled when the soft sounds of the waves mixed with the sounds of her mother's voice.

"Child...do you hear me?" Margarita said. *"Come to me. Come to me, little one..."*

The pleas had grown louder and more insistent. Isabel finally had to stop, drop to the floor and clap her hands to her ears, hoping in vain she would drown out the cries. But soon after that, she called in answer, "Where are you? I need you, Mama! Where are you?"

She tumbled out of the cabin and stood at the top of the dunes. She saw her mother standing in the waves. The surf caught her waist and drew her back as she raised her arms to Isabel, imploring her. *"I'm here,"* she said again and again until Isabel smiled, her body eased, and she opened her arms in return.

"MOM," she said. "I'm coming! I'm coming!" and swam into the high waves.

⁓

Elizabeth had found her way home without help, which in and of itself was a small miracle.

The Edwards' housemaids had never been invited to such an affair and never would be asked again, so they aimed to take full advantage of this invitation. They had worn their Sunday best to the ceremony and were completely enthralled with the party itself. The drama made the day all the more enticing—it fueled their excited gossip for an hour after Mr. Johnson had disappeared. They were atwitter, anxious to compare notes and share details: Who said what? Were any curse words exchanged?

They offered a hundred different theories as to how this all came about. Some believed Joseph to be at fault. He was far too handsome; the girls found it impossible to believe he had character. One girl, a laundry maid who worked part-time for Dr. Edwards, told tall tales about how Joseph had met her on the road one night—a night that was nearly two weeks before he had even arrived in America—and went beyond simple flirtation, leaving all of them to wonder what that could mean.

Some believed Isabel to be mad, and that Mr. Johnson was telling the truth about her. They had seen her over the years; she had a shadowy temperament, and was seen so rarely that some speculated she was chained up in a padded room deep below in the Johnson cellar. There were also the stories of her illness, which scared the women half to death. Was she a contagion? A zombie? They breathed heavily into their kerchiefs when the bolder servants talked on about how she seemed so riled for someone so sick.

Elizabeth suddenly crossed the room with her messy hair, dirty wedding gown, and her makeup all over her face; holding an ax, leaving everyone speechless.

148

Her mother and father paid no attention to her once they had arrived at the reception. She had few friends, and those she had were interested in knowing more about Isabel and what it all meant, which meant avoiding Elizabeth at all costs. She thus found herself alone in a room packed like sardines with strangers.

She took a saddled horse that was tied against one of the far trees. She had no idea whose horse it was; she was too stunned to think about anything other than what she wanted: to escape. She rallied the horse into a full gallop, slowing only for a short spell to watch the surf, take in sea air, and breathe. She was back at the house within the hour.

She tried to tear the wedding dress off, pulling at the neck and back several times, crying out loud in frustration when she got nowhere. Dozens of hooks were in the back; it had taken nearly ten minutes to fasten her up earlier. She stood along the wall by her father's office and tried to slow her breathing as her head rested against the door, still holding the ax. *There is only one way to begin,* she thought: *to know the truth.*

Joseph caught Isabel just as the waves covered both of their bodies. The surf was unforgiving; the strident pulls forceful. The waves kept trying to take them both with long, sinuous draws. Joseph grabbed her hard and pulled her toward him, but she bit him on the arm and he released her, letting her free to swim farther out beyond his grasp.

"Isabel!" he screamed at the top of his lungs. He thrust himself into the tide. Several yards later, he caught her feet and pulled her back. He could feel how hard she was fighting. She writhed and kicked. Her feet wrenched loose once and clocked him hard in the eyes. But he took hold of her each time so that when they reached the shore, they were both limp and exhausted. He kneeled over her. She lay headfirst in the sand as he yelled hoarse, wild threats. "Don't ever, ever leave me again! Do you hear me? You can't—you cannot, ever leave me again! You can't!" He bent his body so that he covered her with his own, his head resting against her back. Touching her was the first moment of peace he had experienced since New York.

He carried her back to the cabin. She fell in and out of consciousness for nearly an hour after that. He was not sure whether she was asleep or had passed out. It frightened him, so he waited with bated breath each time her eyes began to fold. He shook her until she looked up at him and answered a few simple questions that made him confident she was alert. Then he waited again for her to come to the next time she drifted away.

The only time he left her bed was to stand up and walk to the front room, where he gazed at the rifle leaning against the far wall.

"Make him pay," Isabel said simply.

Elizabeth entered her father's office, staring at the large wooden box in the corner. She stood before it and without hesitation, she swung the ax several times, finally splitting the top of the box.

She fell back on her heels when a pile of cash bills spilled out. She sat, staring at it all for a long time. Then she dove her hands down inside the pile, feeling along the bottom of the box, looking for...what? She had come back twice in the past few weeks to look for the letter. but it was nowhere to be found. She wanted to know that it really existed, that she had not imagined all of this, that she would wake, and that the nightmares surrounding her would finally disappear.

She felt about some more, then stopped and lifted her hand out. More bills spilled about the floor as she brought out a worn, yellowed letter. The stamps on its envelope were foreign. She took out the letter, sat back, and began to read:

CARTAGENA, COLOMBIA

March 15, 1880

Mr. Samuel Johnson
New Jersey
United States

Respected Sir:

Warm greetings from Cartagena, your old home. This is to inform you that the body of Margarita was found yesterday—just inside Boquilla Beach. Everything went as planned, and there have been no formal enquiries concerning her death or its cause. We have paid the man who helped achieve your aims well.

On a related note, I hope the woman's daughter, Isabel, is in good health.

Regarding any legal documents to prove a legitimate adoption, and to put an end to your troubles, I'll speak with someone this afternoon. I will write to tell you what is required by the end of this month.

Let me know if there is something else I can do for you.

Always at your service,

HORACIO BUENDIA
Police Commissioner, City of Cartagena
Bolivar, Colombia

"What are you doing, Elizabeth?"

She jumped, the letter dropped onto her lap, and she skittered back some before her father moved inside the room. "Reading," she said when she had found her wits. She raised the letter above her head and waved it. "How did you get this?"

Edwards thought carefully before he answered. "I was pulled long ago into a relationship with your father-in-law that made me...ill at ease. I was handed the letter by mistake long ago by the new postman while arriving at Johnson's house, and I thought it might be about Isabel and that it might be prudent...to take it. It was pure luck, really. It has kept us safe all these years, that letter."

Elizabeth stood and read it again. "You should have taken it to the police, Father. Isabel should not be in his control. None of this—none of this"—tears welled in her eyes—"should have happened." She paused again. "You've used me."

The look on his face bloomed into pure contempt. "Elizabeth. I said yes to his demands. I agreed to do what Johnson asked."

"We will explain that to the police. We can tell them why this happened. They will listen. That's their job—"

"Do you truly believe that? That the world is just? That they would just let me off the hook? I have done nothing right with you. You are as ignorant and stupid now as you were when you were six."

She began to cry harder.

"I'm not going to jail, Elizabeth. I can promise you that." As he walked toward her, she stood and stepped back, banging her legs against the examining the table. "Give me the letter, and go back to your husband," he said. "It's the best chance you have for a life."

She slapped him hard across the cheek. Without even a glance, he slapped her back twice as hard and shouted, "Now shut up and give me the letter!"

Feeling a tinge of blood erupt from her lips, she shoved past him.

He slammed his fists together before following her upstairs to her room. Her door was locked. He began to hurl insults at her through the door, one after the other. She sat on the edge of her bed and listened, wondering how many more slurs he would use before she took a knife to her throat…just so she would not have to listen to another word.

"Elizabeth!" he roared as he slammed his fists harder and harder against the door. *"Give me the fucking letter!"*

She stood, wiped away her tears, stuffed the letter into her corset, slipped past the bath and into the dumbwaiter, eased herself down to the first floor, and ran out the back.

Looking back to see if her father had caught up with her, she crashed hard into a chest. It felt like hard marble, wholly unmoving. Her eyes pinned first to the dried blood that ran in rivers down the vest. She followed the trail upward and drew back when she saw the open gash that ran from Mr. Johnson's eye down the flesh of his cheek, ending halfway down his neck. He was stark white, barely breathing. He appeared to have claws for hands and a beak for a nose. Sweat slicked his wiry hair. He was a specter, just as Isabel had always told her. She tried to push away, but the knife-like points of his sharp fingers dug into her back, holding her in a cage.

"Where are you going, Elizabeth?" he asked quietly.

She felt about to faint. She could not find the strength to utter a sound. She saw Johnson look up as her father stood, framed by the back door.

"She has the letter—from Cartagena, Samuel," Edwards said. "She found it in my office. It's with her, somewhere, tucked inside her bodice, maybe."

Johnson groped her. His hands shoved between her breasts, then down her front. He shifted her right and left. "Where is it?" he asked more than once.

"I destroyed it. The letter scared me. It would hurt my father."

Johnson stopped. She thought he was wondering if she was telling the truth.

"Maybe it's upstairs," Edwards said.

Johnson did not move. He shoved his hand up her dress. She cried in pain, her eyes popped, and he smiled as he punched and punctured.

"Oh, God! Please! No!" she cried out.

"Mmmm." His pleasurable moans ended as he pulled the letter out of her corset and unfolded it. He read it slowly as Edwards stepped toward him. "So you have what you need," he said. "Let's just put an end to all this—"

Johnson looked up just as Elizabeth tried to grab the letter from his hands. They stood together in silence. Elizabeth shook like a leaf. Johnson did not move a muscle.

"What do you plan to do, Elizabeth?" he demanded. "Blackmail me? Is that what you're like? I will give you money if you want. Just tell me—"

"Shut up," a voice demanded. It was strangely calm, with no hint of warfare in its tone. "Just shut up. She isn't going to do anything you ask her. Do you understand that?"

Elizabeth softened her gaze past Johnson's shoulder. Her body began to crumble. As Joseph stepped in, she leaned back on her heels to prevent herself from collapsing.

"Now let her go and turn around," the voice went on.

"What are you doing, Joseph?—or should I ask, what do you *think* you are doing? You haven't learned anything yet!"

"Shut up!" Now Joseph seemed to lose control.

"I looked for your whore everywhere, after you arrived from New York, but she hid well..."

"I told you to shut up!"

"That was my own blood, you fool..."

Johnson felt the rifle at his ear. He loosened his grip, allowing Elizabeth to drop back just enough to be free. A smile rose on his lips and he reeled around, his fist balled, ready to slam it into Joseph's jaw...and then the rifle erupted, blowing Johnson sideways, his body crashing against the nearest tree trunk.

Elizabeth bent over, losing her supper on the grass. Her father walked past her and with utter efficiency took the rifle from Joseph's hands, placed the gun in Johnson's palms, wrapped the fingers around the gun tightly, and aimed the rifle toward the man's half-blown head. Then he tucked the bloodstained letter inside Johnson's waistcoat.

"A decent suicide, it looks like," Edwards proclaimed as he rose.

CHAPTER NINETEEN

Dawn

Isabel dug her heels into the sand as she pulled up her knees and wrapped her arms around them tightly. She felt the breezes shift, and they took her gaze to the north. She pinned her eyes there and then shifted forward. There, just along the horizon line, a figure was etched.

She stood and walked closer to the figure. She could make out his form when she drew her hands to her brow, shading them from the sun. It was Joseph. He was on horseback, and a bulk lay across the back haunches. She began to run toward him and then stopped when she realized what it was. Samuel Johnson's body sprawled across the back saddle. A thin vein of blood trailed down the horse's back legs and along the sandy path.

She looked at Joseph, who stopped, swung his leg over, and led the horse by the reins to where she stood. He did not kiss her; not at first. Instead, he dropped his father's body on the ground and waited. He let his hands caress her hair, then her face, and down along her neck. Only then did he allow his lips to meet hers.

When he did, he felt her move in closer, so that a moment later there was no space between them, not even an inch.

Cartagena, Colombia, 1880

Jacinto, the Giant, rapped twice on the green door. He had waited several days to be paid for the job, and when no envelope arrived, he decided he would enquire.

Mercedes answered, narrowing her eyes slightly. When he stated his name, she said briskly, "I'll tell the commissioner you are here." She watched the man's eyes trace the curves of her body; the lascivious ideas that came to her mind made her queasy.

She opened the door wider a few moments later and allowed him in. "Straight back," she instructed the man with her eyes. With his usual loping gait, he made his way down the tiled hall. She followed him and stopped at the arch that led to the very back, where the open-air veranda met the lush foliage that overgrew the ends of the property.

Here Jacinto paused and glanced briefly at the small stone figure on a low wooden table. He knew it from his grandmother—it was Aztec, a short figure, its stubbled legs raised before the thick cylindrical body. The face was not human—more like a spirit, the eyes closed in sinister repose.

The commissioner was watering plants. He turned toward the giant. "Good afternoon," he said with a smile.

"Good afternoon," Jacinto responded. "How are you?" Then the commissioner heard him mutter under his breath, *"The god of Death."*

"Yes," the commissioner said. He did not need to know what the giant was referring to. "Pre-Columbian—it is quite a valuable work. Did you send the letter to the United States?"

Jacinto nodded. "Yes. I have done all you asked."

"Yes." The commissioner pulled a fistful of gold coins out of his pocket and placed them into the giant's broad, moist palm.

"Yes. Is this your house now?" he asked.

"Yes." The commissioner sounded pleased with himself. "I inherited it—in a fashion. I'm working on fixing it up, before I bring my family. I fell in love with this house since I took my first step in it. Sr. Johnson had to leave without notice, and it suited him to deed it to me. The foreigner's visit to the city was a miracle. It rained gold." He smiled broadly.

They both laughed at once. Then the commissioner offered the giant a smooth taste of aguardiente, and the mood changed. "Mercedes?" he called out. "Can you make us some supper, please?"

They ate too much. It was their habit; they never saw much past the day they were in. When the spasms began to hit them, it was so sudden, neither of them could even stand from the table. Not long, just moments later, the acrid foam filled their mouths. The poison froze both their tongues; blood oozed from their eyes and ears. The giant died first as his lungs punched up into his mouth. He gasped for air and then dropped his head onto his plate, breaking the china in two.

Mercedes stood over the commissioner as he died. She wanted to watch his eyes—they bled copiously across his cheeks. "I put enough in the food to kill ten rats," she said. "Better to be safe, yes?" His head fell back, and the folds of fat stretched across his neck while she stood in front of him. "He wasn't a miracle. He was like a storm who blew us all. But, after all, it did rain gold in Cartagena, didn't it?" She broke a glass against the wooden table and stuck a shard into the commissioner's heart.

When she was sure he was dead, she closed both their eyes before she took the gold from their pockets, tucked the money into her dress, and left the house with all her belongings.

She knew of the boat that would leave the harbor early in the morning and she was determined to embark on it. She would get off on one of the islands, perhaps Cuba, or The Dominican Republic, she didn't know. But she knew she would embark.

THE END

Made in the USA
Monee, IL
11 March 2020